TEN THOUSAND YEARS

by Robert Quicksilver

January 2019

Los Angeles, California

Dear Reader,

Ten Thousand Years is the story of three souls, each with its own individualized nature, who are born, die, and are reborn continuously over a period of ten thousand years. Beginning in their early lives, with rudimentary language and limited conscious awareness, these souls begin creating karmic patterns that play out over their ten thousand year journey. As our heroes incarnate in three-dimensional bodies, mostly on Earth, but also on other three-dimensional planets, their story unfolds.

It is also the story of two celestial beings who are tasked by the Creator to help manage and sustain Creation, particularly the evolution of sentient beings, including our three protagonists.

Finally, and ultimately, it is the story about God, the Creator, the Creatrix, and Their Creation. It is the story of the evolution of cosmos and the ongoing transfiguration of All That Is.

In order to follow their merging and co-merging lifetime patterns, and as a literary tool, I have assigned the letters "R," "S," and "T" as the first letter of our heroes' names in any particular lifetime. In the same way, names beginning with "L" and "A" refer to the two celestial beings, Ladro and Aung, who help the Creator maintain the cosmic evolution and who, from time to time, incarnate in their own three dimensional bodies.

Over a period of ten thousand years, these three souls incarnate again and again and again in different genders, in various familial relationships, and in various historical periods and sets of circumstances, fumbling their way through Creation as their conscious awareness grows slowly. The celestial beings try to guide and inform their evolution, as the Creator watches from the distance.

Welcome to their journey.

Robert Quicksilver
September 2019

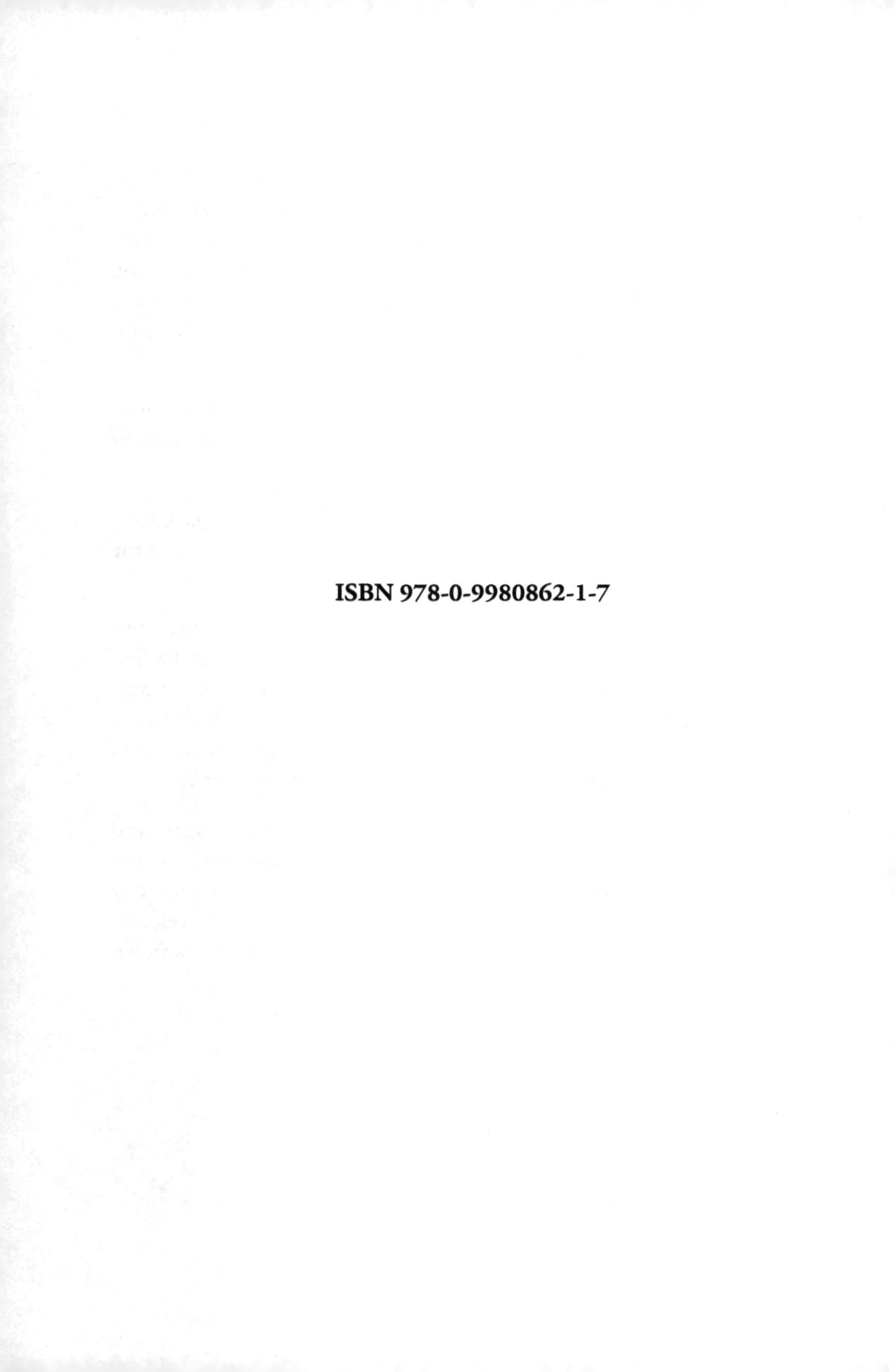

ISBN 978-0-9980862-1-7

Index

Overture

He said, "I want to hold You, make love to You all day."
She said, "You are mine to hold, to dream with while we play."
He said, "You are the moon and stars. I fill You with My Light."
She said, "And I'll become the world, and dance for You all night."

She said to Him, "My Lord of Love, breathe me into form."
He said to Her, "O sweet Divine, in your Heart my Life gets born."
She said, "I shall become the World that you imagine in your mind,"
He said, "And I'll live inside your heart, until the end of time."

He cried to Her, "You are my Life, I cannot say goodbye"
She whispered back, "The aeons pass in the blinking of Thine eye."
He clung to Her, "O Love, don't go. I'll know not what to do."
She said, "Fear not, my Lord, I'll always be with You."

And then She left, reborn as form-
The earth, the moon, the stars above
And living things and life and death
And joy and passion and sacred love.

Now He could only touch Her skin
And sustain Her worlds of beasts and men
And watch the aeons come and go
And wait until Her Dance might end.

Prologue

Ladro is standing near the Generator. This is a series of massive concrete, steel and polymer buildings extending far beyond what the eye can see in all six physical directions. Sitting at its controls, Ladro directs the functioning of Creation, and as its Master Magician, is specifically tasked by the Creator Himself to keep the cosmic engine humming. There are dozens of what can only be called smokestacks rising into the vast Escher-like array with a sweet-smelling purple-gray smoke spewing out their conical tops. Different size pipes and armatures extend at every possible angle. Some are parallel, others cross each other, intersecting at odd slopes with impossible configurations. Some pipes seem to just stop in mid-space. Some seem to wave in and out of position. The whole array is electric and alive with pulsation. It is glowing and the background roar is deafening.

In Ladro's hand is something that almost resembles an old-fashioned calculator, except for the color neon tubes circling around it. He is frantically switching colors, moving buttons and ferociously shaking it. The calculator device itself begins to change shape, becoming round, then oval, then suddenly quiet. All the lights go out. A look of distress crosses Ladro's brow.

"This can't be!" he screams. "I must have miscalculated!"

Ladro shakes the device vigorously. Suddenly, and without warning, the calculator comes briefly back to life as the entire array changes shape. Dark belching clouds appear over one of the utility substations; enormous electric ion particle streams explode out from a particularly intricate pipe array. Large pieces of this impossible superstructure begin to fall away; others collapse inwardly.

"No! No!" screams Ladro again, as more substations black out. He moves into the hub of the main control room and tries to rework the calculator device again by unlocking various switches on the central terminal's quantum matrix display. The Generator seems to be responding. New laser-neon tubes begin to interweave with the main tubes. Holographic quark-sized protonic conductors connect the newly formed tubes. Slowly the negative ion streams decrease. The substations go back online. The massive electric pulsations emanating from the central core remain diluted but unabated. Ladro is relieved but visibly exhausted.

"Whew! That was close. What the fuck happened? I thought I had that continuity equation worked out. Definitely there was no decrease in the universe-wide biological Death count. Definitely, all the dying life forms continued the release of their elemental bi-trionic energy plasma when they died. What could have happened? Why did the Generator go offline like that? Did someone miscalculate the bi-diodic coefficient of the molecular decay?" he screamed at the assembled acolytes.

Ladro reworked the numbers. And he reworked the numbers again. And again. "Let's see. I know the margins are thin, but I only need a micro-fraction of a nana-bot more energy input than output. It's such a small margin to work with. I know it's tight, but the energy output quotient is…" at which point he proceeded to punch a series of enormously long octometric equations into his mega-matrix calculator, "…and the energy input quotient is…." The machine hummed and changed color. "The Generator operates at a perfect efficiency, so that zeroes out…I just don't know what it is. Something is wrong here. This can't be happening. It's impossible. This machine is functioning at its perfect efficiency. There's plenty of original fuel, plenty of recycled Death plasma to get transformed. Nothing is lost. It's not supposed to break down, There's no reason…."

Ladro sat down at his desk and pulled out some handwritten quadratic equations from an old notebook. Something he had transcribed as a rookie agent. He looked from one page to another, then back to the monitor, then back to the transcript. "Let me see…what's this…this shouldn't be here. How did this parallel processor get inside? He told me there wouldn't be any outside influences on the Generator. What's this nasty nanabot that's infiltrating my system? Something's hacking into the core code. What's going on?"

Ladro kept working the formulae while rerouting the direction-of-flow of the ion stream inside the consciousness-matrix, all the while trying to block this invader from harnessing the Generator energy. He was getting very distressed, sweating and palpitating. "The Creator will not be happy. He told me to take care of it, make sure the original burst from His Big Bang was sustained. He said it was very important, something about a promise He had made to someone. He told me that the system was net neutral, that the death and dissolution of one form was the genesis and fuel supply of the subsequent emergent form. No energy lost. And here it is, 15 billion years later and the whole friggin' system is shutting down. The release of the bi-trionic energy at the time of bio-cellular death- the Death constant- doesn't seem to be enough to compensate for the energy drag required to sustain the system wide force field. Maybe the overhead is too high, the inertial dampening too low. Maybe it's this hacker trail from a parallel universe. Maybe the basic assumptions are incorrect. This sucks! What am I going to do?" Ladro asked no one in particular as he glanced over at his acolytes, all sitting in fear and distress just outside the main control room.

A dejected and defeated Ladro sits down on an unpainted bench near the Generator office. Suddenly, out of nowhere, from inside a shimmering strand of etheric silk lattice, the Creator appears. Ladro throws himself prostate before the Creator, who grabs him by the collar and yanks him into a standing posture.

"What's going on here?" the Creator asks Ladro, more for effect than a request for information. Of course, He already knew the answer, knew it would come to this.

"It's a mess! It's a bloody mess! I don't know what happened. It was working fine all these billions of years. And now, now it just seems to have zipped out, stopped working. It just went kaput! I don't know what happened. I've tried everything… Someone's hacking into the core thread…"

Ladro, simultaneously dejected by the reality of the situation, and exalted at being in the presence of the Creator Himself, could only mumble nonsensible mathematical formula.

He went to get his calculator but the Creator said "Put that stupid thing away, Ladro. Listen, this isn't your fault. I had hoped that there would be enough micronic energy recovered from the death of biologic forms to keep the engines stoked indefinitely. I wanted to believe that so much that I disregarded the early warning signs. I didn't want it to come to this. What we have to do now. But She knew. I should have listened to Her. It's very sad."

At which point a huge sorrow crossed the shimmering face of God. The sadness on His face was palpable. In the hundred billion galaxies a wave of sadness overcame all creatures, all inanimate objects, all nescient existence. Some say it rained non-stop for a hundred million years on the water planets.

"Ladro," the Creator began once He had composed Himself, "we will have to modify the basic structural formula for the Cosmic Engine. Instead of the Generator fuel being dependent exclusively on the utilization of the bi-trionic energy plasma released at the death of biologic forms, we will have to introduce this additional code which allows for the development of Sentience, and the evolution of conscious awareness in the evolving bio-matrix on the various inhabited worlds along the Spirals. Once this new triadic code becomes integrated into the underlying universal consciousness-matrix, it will bring a system-wide Sentience into the entire framework of bio-quantum existence. I am transmitting these parameters into your central holographic light matrix so you can download them."

Suddenly, the Creator moved his hands in a specific series of impossible martial art-like gestures. Adding Sentience to the primary consciousness-matrix changed everything. The code for Sentience- wherein the Creation develops Awareness and Knowing of Itself- spread like a tornado of viral wildfires through the multitude of embedded layers inside the consciousness-matrix. In an instant, everything was different.

Ladro, suddenly feeling much better, but still apprehensive, asked "I don't get it. How's this going to work? What will this 'Sentience' do for the Generator and the whole project you assigned me of sustaining Creation?"

Patiently, as if speaking to a little child, the Creator explained to Ladro: "It works like this. As this new code for "sentience" becomes embedded in the underlying consciousness –matrix, the individuated loci of all bio-physical forms will undergo a deep and profound change. All creatures will start to become aware. With an evolving self-awareness in its creatures, particularly the sentient creatures, Creation itself will become Aware."

"Of course, it is the more complex beings, especially the humanoids living on the Outer Spiral Rings, that will be most affected. Sentient animals and even sentient rocks and trees are miracles to behold, but when these stumbling humanoids become sentient, everything in Creation changes."

The Creator went on. "One of the first things that inevitably happens to newly sentient humanoids, when they first start becoming self-aware, is the development of a separate personality and ego-consciousness.

They begin to think of themselves as separate and distinct creatures- separate from Me, separate from Her. The illusion of this separateness, this illusory hook, becomes the basis of a separate ego-consciousness, which causes all sorts of problems and entanglements within the laws of time and humanoid activity."

"The second, and more significant, consequence of this evolutionary change is that the sentients suddenly realize the predictability and inevitability of their own death and the death of everyone around them. This realization changes everything in the fabric of sentient `consciousness."

"And the third consequence of an embedded sentience is the empathic knowing of pain and suffering in oneself and others. And so on: consequences and entanglements too numerous to list. Everything in Creation changes...." said the Creator, as He paused for a moment looking expectantly toward the distance before continuing.

"All this 'new' energy- the raw suffering and enormous malcontent that becomes inevitable with the development of sentient consciousness will become the new additional fuel for the Engine. The Generator, once you have updated some of the input quotients, will use the intense nucleonic strings of this heightened emotional matrix, endemic to three-dimensional consciousness, as fuel for the Engine, lower grade perhaps compared to Death itself, but there will be so much abundance and quantity of this conflicted emotional string energy that we will never run out of fuel. Your fires will burn for aeons!!"

The Creator said all this almost matter-of-factly, as though reciting from a well-rehearsed script. As He stared off into the distance, the sound of the Generator became louder. More tubes and pipes appeared inside the array; new concrete polymer buildings began to spring up in the blackness of space. Moments later, as the revised code was fully set in place, the Creator sat back, pulled a tissue from his breast pocket and wiped His eyes.

Solemn and distressed, almost looking weak and beaten, He stared directly at Ladro. "I thought I could do it. I thought I could sustain this whole Creation with the energy released from death, decay and dissolution only, without having to introduce sentience and the whole tragic consequence. But, alas, She knew it all along. She knew Her heart would have to break a hundred million times. But She insisted. She wanted

Creation to become a knowing of Itself, a knowing of its own existence, a knowing of Her Body. I insisted that we make it work with the plasma energy released at the Death of biologic forms only. "…that this would be sufficient to sustain You," I told Her repeatedly. But that's not what She wanted. "And besides," She said, "who will know if we don't give Creation knowing, who will dance with Me, who will celebrate Your vision with Me, who will cry with Me, who will have joy with Me, who will witness this great and awesome thing that you do with your breath…" And on and on She would go. "Death won't be enough." She knew this would happen. I pleaded with Her not to do it. but Her joy was so great, there was no stopping it. I promised to sustain Her and Her creatures while She danced. She said the only way I could do this was to code an evolving sentient consciousness into the basic engine at the core of the spiral matrix. I didn't want to listen. I pretended that dead and decaying molecules, from the death and dissolution of biologic forms, would release enough micronic energy back into the primal substreams for Her to use. I had hoped that would be enough. I carefully designed the hardware making sure to use and reuse every scrap of micronic participle. Nothing was wasted. It was my Machine, my Creation, my Cosmos. I could make it any way I wanted, make any set of laws that I wanted! And I definitely didn't want this Sentient mess, But She just looked at me. And smiled."

Suddenly, a deep and profound anguish overwhelmed the entire Creation. The new code, redesigned for Sentience, had saturated the consciousness-matrix. It was now endemic throughout the hundred billion galaxies as the Creator continued His lamentation. "Without sentient consciousness the creatures that populate the Creation do not know Time or Death or Love. Now they will know all this and more: desire and craving, and lust and greed. Hatred will overwhelm them, and they will fight and betray each other from one end of the cosmos to the other. That's not what I wanted. But maybe it had to be this way. She said it would come to this. She knew it. And now the stone of sentience has been cast. But there is no joy in this, watching as Her children are born already saturated with dissatisfaction and despair. But it's done now." The Creator mumbled as He again looked off into the distance.

Ladro, no longer feeling beaten by the burnt-out Generator, was suddenly upbeat, even happy. An upgraded calculator appeared in his hand. New input devices appeared on its side, plugged into various ports and docks. He was ready to get back to work managing the Generator, making sure that the flow-through was optimized and the coefficient of the microtronic variation was stabilized and that, generally, the machine was operating with maximum-plus efficiency.

Ladro was busy taking care of his business when, suddenly, the Creator moved His hands in a complicated and impossible way and there, suddenly, standing next to Ladro was a beautiful and glowing celestial being who immediately fell prostrate in front of the Creator. The Creator made him get up. "Aung, my dear son, I am so happy to see you," He said with obvious emotion and enormous generosity. Ladro looked a bit perturbed. He continued. "I thought I would never see you again. I had even hoped I would not see you. But here we are my son, just where we left off."

"My Lord," exclaimed Aung, "I have been gone so long, waiting for you to call to me. I was cast into the wilderness between Creations, without existence. What's happened? Where have You been? Where is She?"

Ladro looked around. She? Does this Aung know who the Creator was talking about just before? How does this Aung know about that? Where did this pretty boy come from anyway?

"Ladro, this is Aung, who I have brought over from a parallel Universe to help get involved with things here." said the Creator very matter-of-factly to Ladro.

"Help with what?" retorted Ladro immediately. "Now that we got this sentient thing coded you said there would be plenty of fuel to sustain the Generator. I don't need any help." Ladro added with not a small amount of pride- and arrogance- in his voice.

The Creator replied. "It's not to help you, it's to help Her. To help Her creatures as they become sentient. I can't just leave them to this impossible suffering that I created. Their cries and lamentations echo through the fabric of Creation and overwhelm Her with sadness. I have to try to alleviate their pain…I have to do something."

The Creator was visibly moved. The molecules of space shuddered. Aung fell down to his knees and laid his head against the Creator's feet, crying profusely. Aung knew what lay ahead; he knew the extent of the inevitable assault on the sentient mind that was about to happen; he knew that a huge tidal wave of incomprehensible pain and suffering was about to overwhelm the consciousness-matrix. He could see fragments of the future, from the smallest tear that a child might shed when scolded by an angry parent to the dark oceans of blood that whole generations of sentient beings will shed when confronted with the hellish consequences of their greed and hatred.

This decision- to recode the universe for sentient consciousness- had huge and enormous consequences beyond the mere fact of sustaining creation. The introduction of sentient awareness into the universal equation changed everything.

It was quiet for a long time.

Ladro was the first to speak. "Who cares! These creatures are only alive for the few moments. Then they die. OK, so now they will have some suffering during their fleeting lifetime. What's the big deal? Who cares about the suffering of these little creatures? We get the energy and the whole Creation goes on. That's what you want, right? Why all these tears, all this crying? All this emotional hysteria doesn't get the energy we need to keep the Generator going. Decay and death, and, ok, now also sentient craving and suffering, give us the energy we need to keep the furnace going. Why are the both of you so upset?"

Aung was about to say something when the Creator signaled to him to stay quiet. The Generator was pulsing wildly. Sentient life rose up out of the fabric of existence in all the sixty-four corners of the universe. What had once been a seamless blanket of hard dense static mineral and rock- which had miraculously become alive with biologic necessity- had now morphed again into a pulsating protoplasm of sentient consciousness.

Aung quietly watched Ladro work the Engine for a few moments and then he looked off into the distance, pain and distress racking his face, as he shuddered and disappeared. The Creator stood there alone. It looked like He was having a conversation with someone, but no one was there. He reached out His hand as though to touch someone, but there was only empty space where He touched.

The Creator stood there for a long time. And then, suddenly, He was gone.

And so, in this way, the seamless, beautiful, and harmonious Creation had become transformed. Additional creases and folds appeared in the fabric of existence as sentient beings began to arise in the sixty-four corners of the universe.

Book I

The Caves

Chapter 1- The Dawn of Consciousness

The last thing Roga remembered, before he died for the first time, was the warm fire in the center of the cave where he slept. He could remember the glow of the fire and the dancing shadow patterns they created on the walls. He could see another person painting blood drawings on the wall. He knew this person; he had always known her. And there was another person sharpening stones and wooden spears in the corner. But mostly he remembered how warm it was.

It had become Roga's task to find the wood for the fire and twice a day he would leave the cave, go down into the river rock and bring back as much wood as he could carry. On the second trip on this particular day, just before the sun moved to the edge of the sky, the ice cracked under where he had been walking and he fell off the rock cliff into the bottom of the river rock. He was badly hurt and unable to move and, despite his cries for help, no one came initially to help him, probably because his family was sitting near the fire, inside the clan cave, unable to hear his him. When they did go out to look for him they found he had fallen deep in the river ravine where the sheer rock walls prevented any rescue. As the sun moved behind the mountain, and the darkness fell onto the river rock, he lost consciousness and died. The last thing Roga remembered was the warm fire. And how he just wanted to be sitting next to the fire with his family.

His sister, Sana, painted his likeness on the wall of the cave. From the neck bone of a wild boar, Toda, his brother, made a small carving which he put beneath Sana's painting. Both painting and carving remain there still. The tribe they were part of left the rock walls the following spring and were all killed in a giant flood that swept down the river rock canyon without any warning. The cliff caves, however, being higher up the rock wall, were untouched and, over time, became covered up with dirt and rock and vegetation. Ten thousand years later they remain undiscovered.

When Roga awoke, he found himself sitting next to the fire, next to someone whose smell he liked, someone who made him feel good, who gave him food. Roga was sitting cross legged on the floor next to his mother's knee as she was skinning an animal that someone else in his cave tribe had killed. Roga noticed a very strange feeling in his body. He noticed that he was sitting there, next to his mother. He often sat there, he somehow knew, next to the warm fire, but something was different this time. He knew that he was sitting there, he saw himself sitting there. As though he had another eye in the corner of the cave watching himself sit there. This perception lasted only a moment and then was gone. Roga felt like he was dreaming but he knew he wasn't. It was very strange. But then it was gone. He wanted to say something to his mother but there weren't any sounds that he knew to describe this experience. Besides his mother was very busy preparing the animal skin and she would get angry if he started to take her attention off of her work. He was happy just to lie there, next to the fire.

Suddenly, a huge person, his father Tama, burst through the cave opening and started grunting and screaming at everyone: "Get up, hurry, the Lbgi are coming. Fast, get up…" But it was already too late. Three light skinned men with blood paint on their faces burst through the cave opening and within a few moments Roga, his father Tama and his mother were lying dead. His sister, Sana, was taken by the Lbgi men to the other side of the rock valley as a prisoner and slave. Finally, when she died, and as she lay there on the floor bleeding to death, she remembered the painting of her brother on the rock wall. But how could that be? She didn't draw on any rock wall. She died then.

Once released from her body, Sana found herself able to fly around. While it seemed that no time had passed from the moment she died on the floor, in fact quite a lot of time had passed. Tamara, someone who she trusted, had grown into a full womanhood in the Fire Mouth tribe at the edge of the great Mahawa Forest. Sana felt compelled to fly into the middle of the tribe's central fire and from there she was catapulted into

Tamara's waiting womb. Was she surprised to find Roga already there! Roga tried to push her away but the trillion molecules had already begun to multiply and Sana's etheric wings were already being threaded into the womb lining. Roga and Sana continued to jostle which made it very uncomfortable for Tamara. As a result, she became very ill and during the entire pregnancy she cursed her situation. Finally the two siblings settled down. During the birth itself, however, Tamara's uterus ripped and as she pushed the new lives out of her body, her own life was also pushed out. She went unconscious just as Roga started crying and bled to death very quickly.

Roga and Sana were looked after by Tamara's mother, an old woman with large eyes, large hands and a loud voice. She was constantly scream-ing at the two young children, often hitting them with her large hand while they were playing outside the clan cave. Her cave mate would usu-ally arrive at the cave entrance just before dark and drop a small animal carcass on the fire, then sit at the cave entrance with his spear in hand, peering out at the bush just outside. Mostly things were quiet and the only problems were getting enough food and staying warm. Roga liked to be warm and it was there, sitting next to the fire that he first noticed the back of his hand. He noticed his fingernails with their short and squared off edges. He noticed his legs, crossed under him, his feet under his calves. He'd never noticed these things before. This was his body he was noticing; he was noticing that he was noticing these things. He looked over at Sana who was also looking at her hands. All together this was very strange.

He kept watching as his mother's mother turned the small animal carcass on the fire, moving it back and forth slowly. He noticed the way she carefully stretched the skin away from the body before she cut at its underside with the sharp rock. He noticed how she grunted and squint-ed with each successive cut, her lips curled tightly with her gnarly teeth protruding from her lips.

She worked very hard and had no time to be distracted by him or his sister. Even now his sister sat away from them, in the far corner of the cave making marks on the wall with the animal blood. He noticed how she carefully dipped the animal tail into the hollowed rock which was filled with blood and then rubbed that onto the wall. Once again he noticed that he was watching her. It made him feel...strange, all this noticing, and he wished for it to go away.

He lay down where he was sitting, his head brushing up against his grandmother's knee and fell asleep. In his dream he saw images of his sister and another man he did not know. In the dream she one day left the clan cave and went off with this other person. Roga woke up with a start and looked in the corner to make sure his sister was still there- which she was- and then fell back into sleep. Roga died soon after when a clan group from across the river violated the blood ring protecting his family cave. Roga tried helping to defend his clan but he was a small boy and was easily thrown down and killed. When he died he suddenly found himself on top of the White Mountain, a very far distance from the Malawa Forest where he had been living. He had no idea how he had gotten there and, more surprisingly, someone named Tama was also there. He instinctively knew this person. He was looking down from the top of the mountain into the village where his sister Sana was now living. She was older than he remembered and she was now living with the man Roga had seen in his dream.

There was a strong urge to go be near Sana, to be around her and he quickly found himself wrapped in a small body inside Sana's womb. He looked to see if Tama was there, having remembered that he had, at one time shared this dark place with someone, but he discovered that he was alone. He felt safe and warm floating inside Sana's womb and almost immediately found himself born into another clan cave. He was very glad to see Sana, and, although he didn't really remember any of this past, he had the strangest feeling that this was someone he knew and that he felt safe.

It went on like this for slightly more than six hundred and fifty terrestrial years as their awareness and experience of life kept increasing. One life after another: bam bam bam. While Sana, Roga and Tama kept switching familial and gender roles, they basically stayed near each other during that whole period. Each time they died they yearned for the continuation of life, craving the experience of life, the desire for flesh, the warmth of the fire. They hungered for experience, for love and touch and smell and feeling.

Roga, generally, was born as a male, usually smaller and slight of build but quick and smart. Tendo was almost always larger than Roga, also mostly in a male body and quite adept as a warrior. He took pride in his devotion and chose every opportunity to battle for the good and the right. Sana was more often born into a female body, fair and beautiful, at once clever and aware. Her artistry is woven throughout history in pottery, on rock walls, in churches, buried in tombs and shrines. And so their journey began.

Chapter 2 The Dye is Cast

Radu had spent his childhood years with Sara, playing in the same weed patch, digging together for roots, throwing rocks at little creatures running to their burrows. They played chase games and tag games; they fought over food scraps; they hunted small lizards together. He's not sure when the smell of her womanhood began to make him uncomfortable. He did remember the first time their eyes made that special contact- the kind of contact filled with meaning and desire. She had been bathing in the river when he and his friends had gone to see if they had caught anything in the small dam they had constructed out of wood and rock. She came running up the path, only half clothed, her long black hair hanging down around the naked part of her body.

Something happened then. He'd experienced being frightened by the wild creatures, especially the Yads, certain of immanent death. He'd been elated and thrilled when he caught his first Paggam and proudly brought it to the cave to show the clan. He'd been in pain many times from serious and not-so-serious wounds. But he never felt anything like this as a wave of fire swept over his entire body. It seemed like it came from out of nowhere and, all of a sudden, he was more frightened than he ever had been. He wanted to run after Sara and take her, but before he could move she was far down the path. The surging fire waned and his normal self returned within a few minutes. His friends were already far ahead and he had to run to get caught up. He felt like he was walking on air. It felt good. It felt strange. He noticed how good he felt and how much he liked that feeling. From that day on his life was different. As it turned out, not only was this life different but hundreds of lives spanning thousands of years would be different.

Immediately after the incident on the waterpath, life changed for the clan. The Wooden Clan which had lived in the woods, high up the mountain that belonged to the great river, moved down to the river. Winter had arrived earlier than expected on the mountain and the Wooden

Clan was not prepared. The early snow buried their planting field. The animals were staying in their lairs and they had not stored enough meat in their caves. Hungry and angry they trekked down the mountain and onto the flatter- and warmer- meadows. As a clan, they were very threatening and all the tribes were prepared to fight them. However, the elders of the tribes met together and it was agreed that they would combine the different clans. This would make them all stronger and more able to ward off the predators as well as other clans that might want to take the limited food that was available. They became known as the FishWood Clan and, because of this joining, they had become the largest and strongest clan-tribe along the great river.

One member of their clan, Tendo, was a young boy like Radu and they became friends quickly. They spent the next several years growing into manhood and soon became members of the hunting party that went off in search of food for the combined clan. During these few years, Radu scarcely saw Sara at all though when the time came Radu knew he would take Sara up the river to the tree where the shaman said that babies come from. He would take Sara as his mate. But for now he had more important things to do, being taught the ways of the clan and training to be a hunter, bringing fresh meat to the FishWood Clan every day.

Tendo did not go hunting every day. Often he would stay by the river with the fishing boat. How strange it was, Radu thought, that he, from the Fish Clan had become a hunter in the Wood and Tendo from the Wood Clan had become a fisher on the River. What Radu didn't know was that during those days, Sara and Tendo had begun spending time together in the hidden coves along the river. Tendo never said a word to Radu about his meeting and mating with Sara.

At about this time, in the year that the red fever disease was making everyone sick and causing many to die, Sara had moved into a cave much closer to Radu to live with another family clan that included three young children who had become orphaned when both their parents died from the red fever heat. Radu started going over there, helping Sara care for the young children. They were both very excited to be with each other again and soon thereafter they consumated their childhood longings.

Many moons later, Tendo, who had been traveling with the Fish-clan elders upriver to find new fishing ground, returned on the afternoon before the first ice storm. Radu didn't see him return, but heard the whispering around the clancaves. He didn't give it much thought. All he could think about was Sara and finishing his work cleaning hides so he could go to Sara's adopted cave and fulfill the burning desire which was racking at his loins every second. When he finished his work, he ran as quickly as he could to find Sara but she was not there. The rest of her adopted clancave was there but Sara was nowhere to be seen. Dejected, Radu decided to walk over to the river to see if he could find his friend Tendo and hear any tales from the long boat journey. There was some flurry of activity near the boat, but he did not see Tendo anywhere. He walked past some of the elders and asked them if they had found anything good. They smiled, nodded their heads and went on with their work of putting the boat in a safe place. Some of the younger men were helping, but none of them looked up as Radu asked them about the trip. "I decided their strange behavior was due to their long trip and thought nothing more about it," he would much later recall. As he was walking back to the caves he heard a booming voice from the river hut. He was sure it was Tendo and decided to go say hello to him. As he got closer he also heard a woman's voice.

Tendo and Sara were in the corner of the river hut rolling around the earthen floor. Tendo would grab Sara, who would try to get away. He wouldn't let her. Then he jumped on top of her and joined with her forcefully. Sara was crying and screaming and kicking. Then Tendo would roll off and Sara would jump up, kick Tendo in the ribs, and then jump on him. Again they would join and then Sara would jump off and Tendo would grab her and on like that. Radhu couldn't believe what he was seeing. Once he realized what was going on, his pain and hurt translated into anger and he started breathing very heavy and in gasps. Within minutes he erupted like a volcano. First his hands began to shake, then his heart began pounding like the hunting drum. Below his heart, just above his navel, it seemed like a giant rock had crashed down and exploded. He was filled with rage; sweat began to pour from his brow. Anguish filled with hate erupted in his mind. He had no words to describe these exploding feelings, and, sweating and panting like a wild animal, he burst through the door. He must have looked like a wild Yad in the middle of a kill because Sara and Tendo both looked at him with terror in their eyes.

He lunged at Tendo intending to grab his throat and choke him but Tendo was stronger and easily threw Radu to the ground. Radu got back up, consumed with rage and exploding waves of violence and hatred.

Shaking uncontrollably, he lunged at Tendo again. This time Tendo hit him with a rock and, perhaps unintentionally, killed Radhu on the spot.

Radhu's last mind moments, as he was falling unconscious to the ground, were thoughts of hatred and revenge, feelings of pain and rage and, though he did not yet know the word, betrayal.

Chapter 3 After the Dawn

He woke up quickly. The wind was howling outside and instinctively he looked at the embers in the fire pit to see if he could make a fire. Rika was surprised to see the fire already going. Who would have made it? He was even more surprised to see so many people kneeling around the fire, eating large sections of what seemed like an enormous Lobsom. While he didn't recognize anyone in specific, Rika felt like he knew many of the people. Sitting closest to the fire, the eldest person there, was someone he knew very well and he knew he hated this person. He didn't know what to call this overwhelming feeling and he just sat there, in terror and distress, filled with hate and loathsomeness. Why he hated this person wasn't clear. He looked around and immediately noticed the walls filled with images painted with Yad and Lobsom bloodand with FireClan warriors surrounding each animal. Next to the man he hated was a woman with a round face and long black hair. He wanted to get close to her, crawl into her lap, suckle and be warm but he was afraid of her.

Suddenly these two people started screaming at each other. The man would come over to the woman, trying to grab her by her hair, but she resisted and spat at him. They screamed angry words at each other that Rika did not understand. Finally the man threw her to the ground and ripped at her animal skin. Rika started to go over to help her but the man kicked him away.

He crawled back to the fire pit and sat there staring at the fire. Rika fell asleep just then and the next thing he remembered was when he was a young warrior and the search party had seen a group of young Lobsoms not too far from the clancave.

It was during this particular hunt that a Skrikaw tail whipped him before he could move away. The tail itself didn't do much harm but as

Rika recoiled backward he fell onto a pointed boulder. His head cracked open instantly and he died right there.

Chapter 4 The Battle Begins

When Rikko woke up, the first thing he saw was the guard standing over him, watching his every move. He knew he was in great danger and closed his eyes immediately so as not to have the guard realize that he was awake. He tried to remember where he was and how he had gotten there. He saw images of fierce fighting, death, and destruction. He somehow knew that he was the brother of the chief of the WaterRock clan and he had been captured by the strange-looking boat people who, one day, appeared from nowhere and attacked his tribe. Nearly everyone had been killed but, for some reason, his life had been spared and now he found himself a prisoner, lying helpless on the dirt floor of his father's hut.

Suddenly, an unknown person, smelling foul with the odor of rotting fish, came in and kicked him in his ribs. "Wake up you piece of shit" this person scowled in a broken tongue. "Wake up or I will cut your eyes out…cut your ears off, break every bone in your body, one by one. Wake up!" he scowled again while kicking Rikko harder, snapping several ribs. The taste of blood came to his mouth as he opened his eyes and glared back at his enemy.

"Tell me where they are and I will let you live you piece of shit" screamed the captor. Then, suddenly, the captor pulled out a jagged stone knife and in one swift action cut Rikko's ear off close to his head. "Tell me now !" he demanded as blood poured from his head and he began to vomit. "Tell me or I will cut your other ear off," his captor screamed as he brought his knife to within inches of Rikko's remaining ear.

"I tell you I don't know- after the attack everyone scattered…I don't know where they went, I saw them running and then someone hit me on the head. I tell you I don't know," Rikko pleaded between his coughing and vomiting blood.

Immediately his captor moved the knife from Riko's remaining ear to his eye. "Your last chance," screamed the captor, "tell me or you will die!" Several more minutes of this went on, as Rikko was cut, pierced, and violated in all parts of his body. He gladly suffered these pains and endured the blows as he continued to protect their secret hiding place. The intensity of his beating increased: blood was pouring out of his wounds, his bones were broken and his head was smashed. He had no resistance left. The pain was unbearable. They would never find her, he said to himself. She's probably escaped from there. If he told them where they were they would leave him alone, he hoped.

He would come to regret this weakness, this betrayal, but in the moment he felt he had no choice. Sobbing and bleeding, curled up in pain and agony, he told his captor where his sister had run off to, the secret cave at the base of the square mountain, on the other side of the river rock. He immediately regretted having said this as his captor laughed and motioned to the guard to kill him, which the guard gleefully did with a sharp lance through his heart. Broken and dying, he remembered thinking how sorry he was for betraying his sister, regret filling his mind as his body convulsed one last time.

The boat people moved upriver to the location beaten out of Rikko. There they found the remaining WaterRock tribe, including his sister. All were killed except for her who was taken as a prize for the boat people's leader, a warrior named Tarack. Tarack was pleased when this girl was brought to him. His appetite for viciousness and barbarity saw no bounds and she survived only several days of this brutality. Her body was left behind when Tarack and his warrior tribe travelled north.

Chapter 5 In Between

I woke up quickly. Next to me me was my mother's sister, Mala, who I had not seen in a long time. I always thought she went off with her mate from `Brglo to establish their own clancave. Needless to say, I was surprised to see her.

"Doya, Mala" I said weakly.

"Doya Roga" she answered back. "What are you doing here?"

"I don't know. We were out hunting and I remember getting whacked by the Scrimshaw tail and then....and then I wake up here and you are standing over me. Where have you been? How did you get here? This is not my father-cave. Where am I?"

"Mala?" Strangely, Mala disappeared as I was talking. I found myself alone in a strange room. The fire was dim but warm and the smell was familiar. This was not Tendo's cave but it was similar. Meat hung in the corner; the walls were streaked with dried blood and in the corner were furs and skins waiting for the ice time. The entrance to the cave was a few feet away. I got up to go outside and look but as I neared the entrance, the entire rock exploded with light and my mind dissolved into an ocean of warm water. I felt like I was in the lake my mother used to wash me in. She would hold me high toward the sun, then drop me into the water. Then she would scoop me up, hold me up to the sun again and again drop me into the water. I'd be scared at first, but soon the game became exhilarating. It felt like that now, except that my mother was not there. I was alone, yet the light all around was so similar to that sun light that I expected to be dropped again. I hung there in breathless anticipation, for what seemed like forever.

Before too long I felt like I was being dropped back into the water, only this time there was no one to scoop me out. I must have stayed under the water for way too long because I blacked out. The next thing I remember was looking up at Tendo who seemed older and meaner than I remembered. I looked around for my mother, Mala, but I couldn't see her. In the corner of the cave, cowering like a scared animal, was Sara, my sister. Tendo was screaming at Mala who came over to me and put a fur skin on my body and then went back to the fire. I tried to call to her but I could not reach up to get the sound out of my mouth. I fell asleep then and I don't remember anything after that.

Chapter 6 Lamro Pays a Visit

I don't remember anything for a long time. I do remember one life time, though, when Tendo and I were sisters. Sara was our father. Our mother had died during my childbirth and we lived in the cave of my mother's brother. His name was Lamro. He was a very large and grotesque man who would rape my sister and I whenever he wanted to. We hated Lamro and lived with fear every day that he would eye one of us and before nightfall we would be beaten as he forced himself on us.

Sara, our father, had lost an arm to a wild Lobsom and could not hunt. He was at the mercy of Lamro, who was providing food and shelter to his family. We lived in fear all the time- slightly less when he was gone but continuously when he was in the cave. I would rather have died at the hands of the Yad and had my eyes eaten out then smell the scent of Lamro. Hate boiled up everyday in the anticipation of Lamro coming back to the clancave after hunting. He would immediately grab one of us. Why did my father let this happen? Why doesn't he do something? I hated my father for letting this happen. I hated my sister, for not fighting back.

One day, when Lamro was sleeping inside the clancave next to the fire, I saw Tendo sneak up next to him with a large rock and was about to smash his head. Our father, Sara, was cowering in the corner watching him. Stupidly- and I've never reconciled why, I screamed out. Lamro woke up in an instant, grabbed Tendo's hand and threw her down to the ground as my father and I cowered in the corner. Lamro smashed her in the face until she was bloody and unconscious, as my father and I looked on helpless. Then Lamro dragged her to the corner and abused her repeatedly. Tendo screamed and cried. Sara and I stayed in the other corner and after many hours of cowering in fear, we fell asleep.

The next day, finally, Sara completed Tendo's plan and smashed the same rock into Lamro's head, over and over again, until he was quite dead. I did not scream out this time as we rejoiced in Lamro's death. At the same time we were afraid for our lives and, especially, the life of Tendo, who lay unconscious in the corner of the cave. How I could possibly have been so stupid as to alert Lamro I never figured out. Could I have hated Tendo that much that I would sell him out to the Devil?

I don't remember anything much after that.

Chapter 7 More Fuel to the Fire

Toga was smiling as he put the cat skins in a pile near a back corner of the clan cave. He knew his pile was the largest of any member of the tribe and he knew that because of it he would become the next clan leader when the old rock thrower, who was now the head of clan, died. And the sooner the better, thought Toga. His tribe had not gone to battle in a very long time and the other tribes were taking more and more of the hunting ground that Toga, and his warrior brethren, needed to patrol for new cat skins. The old clan chief, Movdak the rock thrower, was leery of Toga and the other young warriors and was always watching for signs of rebellion.

In the meantime Sadak, Movdak's eldest son, was also accumulating his own bundle of cat skins for the inevitable day when he and Toga would battle for the right to be clan chief. Sadak knew that in any direct battle with Toga he would get beaten, due to Toga's size and strength. So Sadak and his followers devised a plan to steal Toga's cat skins: without the skins Toga could make no claim to be clan chief. Originally they thought to steal them and add them to Sadak's bundle but they soon realized that that might be obvious to the entire clan and would shame Sadak. Not that Sadak cared about being shamed; he only cared about getting to be clan chief and he wanted that more than anything. Let everyone see how great he was! He didn't understand what his friends were trying to protect him from.

"Sadak," they pleaded, "If everyone sees that you have stolen the skins, your rule will have no honor and none will obey you," they said over and over. But Sadak didn't get it. He didn't even understand what the word 'honor' meant.

"Kill Toga and take the catskins. Throw his bones into the bone pit. Bring me the skins and we will see who is the next clan leader!" screamed Sadak at his friends. And they were afraid, for Sadak would stop at nothing to get his father's seat at the fire. And so his little group of friends plotted the taking of the skins and the killing of Toga.

One of the warriors in Sadak's circle was named Roc. He listened to this plot with high hopes and expectation. This was his chance he thought- it would be his opportunity. With swift action he would be able to accomplish his life long dream, the dream he had over and over again since his first memory in the clan cave, next to the fire pit. His dream to be clan chief and hold all the power so he could do whatever he wanted. He would kill both of them, steal both their skin bundles and proclaim himself the new and all-powerful clan leader. Immediately a plan took shape; he knew he had to act with haste, and very carefully. He had to make it seem that these two- Sadak and Toga- had killed each other. No one could suspect Roc. He would have to appear, after the killings, with his bundle of skins, which was substantial, after all, and become the only person still alive who had the skins and the ancestry to lead the tribe. After all, he thought, if Movdak hadn't killed the brother of his father, Roc would have been in line for clan leader instead of Sadak and, certainly, instead of Toga. So it was correct what he intended to do: take revenge, get even, take what was his, restore honor to his clan tribe and become clan leader.

And so it was that one morning he snuck into Toga's clan cave and slit Toga's throat with one slice of the sharp skin-cleaning rock he had stolen from Sadak's fire pit, which he then left there, next to the lifeless body of Toga. Roc was unexpectedly overjoyed in his blood lust and relished the killing of Toga. With increased confidence he stole the sharp wood arrow from Toga's wall and took Toga's cat skins to the edge of the mountain and threw them down into the great dark crevice on the edge of the mountain that had no bottom.

Then he went over to Sadak's fire pit and waited. Within minutes, one of Toga's wives came running out screaming, holding Sadak's skin rock and yelling curses at Sadak. Just as Sadak bolted out of his cave hut, Roc snuck in and mercilessly stabbed Modak in the heart with Toga's spear head. He ran out into the crowd and when he got to where Sadak was standing he speared Sadak from behind with his own cat killer spear, yelling for revenge against Sadak's clan for the killing of Toga, screaming the death chant in a deep and unholy voice as the entire clan looked on in shock.

As the day passed, it looked to everyone that Toga had killed the clan chief in an attempt to gain the central seat at the clan fire. Then Sadak, in revenge, killed Toga. Then Roc, in an act of justice for Toga had killed Sadak. When the cat skins were brought to the fire pit, it was clear Roc had the largest bundle. And in a unanimous show of support, and perhaps in fear, Roc was looked upon as new clan chief, owning the central fire pit, and possessing the triple feather.

And Roc ruled ruthlessly, slowly killing the friends of Toga and Sadak by sending them into futile battles against the Bear clan. He ruled this way for 11 years until death came from the rotting fever that had swept down the ice world into their river valley. Roc's death was painful and prolonged. He was very afraid and didn't want to die. And well he should be. Needless to say, Tendo and Sara were waiting.

Chapter 8 Blame

"Are you crazy?" screamed Tendo. "What do you think you were doing down there?"

"You started it, you arrogant son-of-a-bitch., you started it when you smashed me with the rock!" screamed back Roga. "You deserved everything coming to you"

"Well you stupid twit, don't you see what you've done now!?" yelled back Tendo in a final exasperation as he began to shimmer and fade.

"Sara, you tell him, I did it to get even, so he could feel what it was like, Sara, tell him, please…" implored Roga to his beloved Sara.

"Stay away from me. Leave me alone. You murderer. You and your stupid obsession!" Sara retorted dismissively as she, too, shimmered and faded.

Roga was left all alone, alone with his anguish and despair, alone with the pain of knowing he had lost the only thing he had ever truly wanted. Ladro came up to him, quite happy.

"Well done, my boy," he said. "Don't let them bother you. You did a great job down there."

Roga began to shimmer and fade. He lost the thread of continuity and went off into a deep sleep.

Chapter 9 Causes and Consequences

Not all those early lives were filled with violence, hatred, betrayal, fear, and despair. There were so many lifetimes, one after the other. Sometimes we would die young, sometimes we would die old. Sometimes we died suddenly, sometimes the death was excruciating and slow. At some point in those lives we would find each other and, for a short time, sometimes, at different times, we might be happy.

That's not to say there were not more betrayals- there were. That's not to say there was not more desire for control- there was. But all in all those thousands of years spent in the caves gave us a full- if raw- taste of what it was like to be alive.

And I loved it. I yearned for it. I craved for another body. I begged to be returned each time. No matter what the circumstances I wanted another spin on that wheel. Of course I wanted to get even with Tendo. Of course I was hopelessly obsessed with Sara. Of course I wanted to be powerful and have everything there was to have, possess everything there was to possess.

Could I put up with the negative conditions, the huge disappointment I would always be left with, never achieving any lasting happiness? You bet I could. Could I put up with the pain and suffering I experienced each time I was alive? Definitely. Could I watch my precious Sara betray my love time and time again? I could endure all this and more. I wanted life so much. I would die, my body would die, my senses were gone, but the yearning fire continued unabated. I was hungry for life, for experience…for power and control. Sometimes I would jump into a new body even before the old one was completely dead. We've all seen old people like this, where a body still survives but there seems to be no occupant.

In this way I was continuously reborn for ten thousand years. On world after world, lifetime after lifetime, desperate for experience, mesmerized by life, desire pounding at my body and mind, running after my soul mates any way I could.

Book 2
China

Chapter 1 Getting Situated

San-Way woke up from her afternoon nap just a little grumpy. She had been cooking all morning and cleaning all afternoon and then, when she could finally stop working, she sat down and fell asleep immediately. No one was in the house. Her husband, Ran-Way, was in the rice field with their two of their sons. One daughter was married to the peasant Chen and lived on the other side of the river. The river was so wide at the bend where it met the town, that Chen's village- and her daughter- might well have been on the other side of the great mountain that rose behind them and cut off the late afternoon sun. Her house- house being a polite description of their bamboo shack- was in the afternoon shadow now, as she awoke from her nap, and this further made her grumpy- and a little cold. She noticed how her hands were gnarled and rough and looked at them with disgust. She remembered as a child how her hands were soft and silken, how she liked to paint beautiful scenery on the clay pots, how much everyone in her family thought she should present them as gifts to the Regent. But life came in the middle of that and she wound up in an arranged marriage to this stupid peasant, Ran-Win.

It wasn't fair, she thought, that after working and struggling for forty years, she had to work as hard each day as the day before. The Regent, Lin-Pan, a greedy and spiteful man, had raised their tax steadily year after year and now, even with the good luck of a string of wet seasons, the rice yield barely gave them enough food after they had paid the 1/3 tax to the Regent. If only her sons would marry. Then she could get some help in the house; she wouldn't have to do all the cooking. Her thoughts rambled on. If only Ran-Win had not hurt his hand in the Regent's army, he would still be in Lin-Pan's guard. Then they wouldn't have to struggle in the field each day, but would be living on Lin-Pan's estate. If only her father had betrothed her to May-Tray instead of Ran-Win, she wouldn't have to think about these things at all. May-Tray had become the Regent's chief guard after he saved the Regent from drowning in the flooded river. If only her father's father had moved them all to the capital during the great famine 50 years before, she wouldn't have to be in these wretched fields at all. She could have married a tradesman or, if lucky, the son of a landowner. Then she would be in charge of a real household, instead of being merely a peasant's wife. And a maimed peasant at that.

Her mental ramblings went on. The wife of a peasant! And what a useless peasant he was. If she were him she would have kept the extra rice they grew instead of giving it away to the beggars and priests. If she were him she would have kept the bag of coins from the traveling merchant when they found him dead on the side of the road that winter morning a few years ago. Instead her husband went and told the village priest who took the money.

Her mind went on like this for some time until darkness began to fall. She quickly got up and put the food on the table. They would be home any second and would want to eat immediately, drink that wretch-ed rice wine and then fall asleep. She would have to clean up their mess and get the kitchen ready for the morning meal. What she didn't know was that this was to be her last night alive. That night, San-way died in her sleep when her stomach lining broke and the digestive juices spilled into her bloodstream.

Ran-Win was surprised to see her in bed when he woke up that next morning. She should have been milking the skinny goat and getting their breakfast ready.

"Get out of bed you fat and lazy pig." He screamed as he pushed her off the bed where she fell bluntly onto the earthen floor. He went over and kicked her once, realizing then that she was quite dead. He had no remorse for screaming at her and was actually glad she was dead. He kicked her again. Now he could have a peaceful life, eat and drink as much as he wanted, bed anywhere. Then he thought of his sons. He didn't have to take care of them, he thought. He called to Tan-Pai, his eldest son.

"Get in here and take this ugly thing away. I'm rid of her at last."

Tan-Pai, who loved his mother, notwithstanding her coarseness and intolerance, not so secretly hated his father for his insensitivity and total lack of caring. He vowed and swore revenge but his thoughts of hatred and revenge were buried by the weight of the circumstances.

His drunkard father was old and sick and died within the year. His remaining sisters would marry and move to another village. His younger brother was simple, even stupid, and would never be able to care for himself. It was up to Tan-Pai to manage this family, a family whose center had been held together through his mother's fierce determination and anger.

His sisters married the year after and Tan-Pai was able to provide them a small dowry of chickens and bedding. He himself married the following year. His new wife, San-Win, came from across the river where her father, also a farmer, had given them several sheep as a wedding dowry. San-Win would shear and weave these skins into beautiful jackets which had found their way into the Regent's noble house. This had given them a small amount of notoriety (as well as some extra silver.)

San-Win, of course, did all the domestic chores and so had less and less time for spinning and knitting. Her knitting time decreased even further when she had her first child and, as was the custom, they named the baby Ran-Way after Tan-Pai's father. They couldn't have known at the time just how many of Ran-Way's qualities the young daughter had inherited. They tried to love the little child, but the child herself, though very bright, was not very friendly and, as she grew older, she pouted more and more, and kept to herself more and more. By the time she was of age Ran-Way was an angry young woman who was constantly fighting with everyone, disturbing the harmony of the entire village. Other children wouldn't play with her and as she grew older even her parents did not want to be around her. Tan-Pai never liked the young girl and found every opportunity to brutalize her. The girl's mother, San-Win, tried to protect her but was unable to intercede between the two of them.

Ran-Way left home when she was fourteen and wound up as a lesser concubine in service of a brutal warlord nine days' journey from her birthplace. No one knew what happened to her and everyone assumed she had died.

Chapter 2 The Regent's Personal Slave

But Ran-Way had survived. In the brutal and callous world of the warlord she fought like a wild dog. Though obviously female, she acted more masculine then like a vulnerable girl. And the warlord liked this quality in her: more than once she attacked him with a knife when he was drunk and violent. He beat her, attacked her and she attacked him back. In this way she found favor in the house of the warlord. Her misanthropic attitude kept her separate from the wives but her aggressive tendencies, when put to use in the bed, kept her alive.

One day the Governor, who ruled from the top of Snow Mountain in the east, came through the warlord's village. The warlord, as a gesture of generosity, gave Ran-Way to the Governor as a gift. The Governor, once he realized how much trouble she was, gave her to his brother, Tomika.

Slowly, over time, Tomika made Ran-Way his favorite concubine. She was like a wild animal. At first, she was cold and hard, but Tomika kept after her and slowly she became adjusted to this life, always expecting to be beaten and raped.

It was a very big surprise when she discovered she was pregnant. The herbs the shaman had given her apparently had not worked. She knew she could not keep it secret but what was she to do? Probably they would kill her and the unborn child. So she was not very surprised when, one night, Tomika confronted her.

For some inexplicable reason he felt sorry for Ran-Way and, against his better judgement, decided to keep her and the baby. This illegitimate male child, Sang-toh, was brought up on the periphery of the court, was always looked down upon and constantly ridiculed and humiliated for the several deformities he was born with, particularly the clubbed arms and feet which became more pronounced as he got older. He was treated like a slave and taught to do the most menial of chores: cleaning the waste from the animal and human slave pens. He always smelled of feces and no one would go near him- the illegitimate and deformed son of the Governor's brother's personal whore slave. Only his mother, Ran-Way, had any love for him- and not that much, really- and Sang-toh lived in an underworld of depravity and disgust. Finally, he was slain by a soldier who caught him stealing food.

Ran-Way herself died several years later. The three of them met again in the afterworld, throwing epithets and incriminations at each other from one end of the star system to the other. "You disgusting this and you greedy and hateful that." They lunged for each other and would have killed each other on the spot were it not for the fact that they were already dead.

Chapter 3 A Choice Not Made

Suddenly, they found themselves born again. Once again they didn't recognize each other and continued in their old ways.

Ra-Wa was born into Tang-toh's family fifteen years before the invasion of the Waima tribe into what used to be the peaceful village of Hangzhou in a very remote part of western and northern China. Ra-Wa's only memory of this life was of him and his father running away from the village. His father, Tang-toh, had managed to escape the Waima warriors by breaking through the rear of their bamboo tent. Unfortunately, Ra-Wa's mother did not make it and she was brutally slaughtered just 5 feet from Ra-Wa when a bludgeon smashed against her head. Ra-Wa escaped, just barely, as his father grabbed him and ran into the woods behind their house. Several others of their village escaped and they gathered at the mouth of the water cave, up the river from the village.

Ra-Wa, in distress, filled with hate and anger, confronted Tang-toh. "Father, how could you leave mother there, to be slaughtered by those butchers," he cried once they had reached the water cave. "You could have grabbed her, saved her, tried to help her…" cried Ra-Wa as his voice trailed off in tears and grief.

"If we had waited any longer we would both be dead as well," replied Tang-toh.

"Better to be dead than have left mother behind in the hands of the barbarians," responded Ra-Wa. Just then Ra-Wa noticed the movement of the trees behind his father and in that same moment a Waima warrior jumped out and smashed his large mallet against his father's head. Suddenly there were Waima all over the place and one by one they slaughtered everyone who was left, including Ra-Wa.

Chapter 4 The Rice Farmer

Ruo-jian, as head of his household in the far western valley of Xing-ho, had little concern for the wars taking place in the distant east, far away from his little village. Thus it came as a big surprise one day when a band of warriors marched through their dusty village, demanding food and women. They appeared at Ruo-jian's small hut in the late afternoon, one spring day, after he and his two sons had come in from the rice fields after a long day's work.

The warrior leader, Captain Tai, was a large and brusque man who came into their hut and sat down at the small table in the middle of the room. The table was low and Tai sat down at the same spot that Ruo-jian usually sat at. Ruo-jian's wife, Shing, who had been cowering in the corner, came out from behind the paper wall, bowed respectfully, and asked the captain if he wanted any tea or perhaps she could prepare some food for him or his soldiers. Ruo-jian was surprised at the forwardness of his wife, who was usually shy and quiet, especially around strangers, but was glad when he saw a smile on the face of the Captain.

Tai said yes to the tea for himself and his 2 assistants. They sat there quietly for several minutes when suddenly, Tai stood up, pulled out his sword and, without warning, pierced it through the heart of Ruo-jian who died quickly on the hut floor. Tai told his assistant to take the two sons, who had been hiding in the corner, and conscript them in the Emperor's army. The four of them quickly left the hut.

Ruo-jian's wife, Shing, was sobbing uncontrollably over the bloodied body of her husband when Captain Tai beckoned her to come to him. "You will come to me, either of your own, or because you are afraid of being beaten, but you will come to me." In shock, crying hysterically, and yet strangely captivated by this Captain Tai, Shing slowly crawled away from the body of her dead husband and cowered in front of Captain Tai.

He lifted up her chin and she looked fiercely into his eyes. She could see her future written there but it was a future she didn't want. She would rather die next to her husband then be taken into slavery by this barbaric Captain.

Shing kept several knives in the drawer for carving the meager meat from their skinny pigs. She stood up, and at first it appeared that she was acquiescing to his demand, but as she was coming closer to the table, she suddenly went over to the drawer, pulled out the longest of the knives and thrust it into her own heart as powerfully as she could. She fell over and landed on top of Ruo-jian and died within minutes.

Tai kicked them both once, then left the hut. He and his soldiers, who had taken whatever provisions this small village had assembled, then left the town, setting fire to several buildings on their way out.

Chapter 5 The Swordsmith

In this lifetime, Tran was an accomplished swordsmith in the northern town of Kofang. His specialty was crafting the beautiful brass metal plating used by the soldiers as armor. In that militaristic society, a renowned swordsmith and armor maker was considered one of the elite of the society. Suti was a member of the Empress's Court. Rikava was a tradesman who bought and sold weapons and in this way had become friends with Tran.

Rikava had been secretly selling Tran's swords and armor to one of the Empress's enemies, the fierce Dogen clan on the other side of the White River Valley and two days journey to the north. Tran was not aware of where the weapons were going, only that Rikava picked them up every second moon and gave him bags of precious gems in return.

One day, a young woman appeared at the court of the Empress, a courtesan named Suti, granddaughter of one of the Emperor's ministers. Immediately Rikava became captivated by the smooth curves of her face, the soft roundness of her lips. During an afternoon ceremony for a visiting Prince, Suti and Rikava happen to be near each other when Rikava notices that Suti is looking at him and, at least from Rikava's perspective, is smiling seductively. Well, one moment leads to the next and, despite a great fear that surges in Rikava's heart, he goes over and begins to talk to her.

At another palace event, Rikava notices that Suti is wearing a necklace made of the exotic jade that Rikava had brought back from Dogen in payment for the swords. When asked where she got such a beautiful necklace, Suti tells him that it was a present from the Swordmaker Tran. Suddenly very unhappy and distressed, Rikava asks Suti what her intentions are with Tran, whereupon she smiles and blinks her eyes in a demure and shy manner. Rikava is shocked. His muscles begin to tighten as he suddenly finds himself angry and fearful. For no apparent reason his lips begin to quiver.

The next day when he visits with Tran, he learns that Suti's parents, with the permission of the Empress, have betrothed Suti to Tran. Rikava is suddenly beside himself as the fierce jealousy and anger resurfaces. They begin drinking Tran's rice wine and, over the next several hours, they get drunk,

Tran begins telling his friend how happy he was about the proposed marriage. The anger that had been reignited in Rikava reemerges suddenly after their third cup of the rice wine. In his drunk stupor, Rikava professes his own love for Suti and challenges Tran to a duel. Tran, who is much stronger and the far better swordsman, begins laughing hysterically, until Rikava grabs his own sword and attempts to go at Tran. Tran easily evades the attack and throws Rikava to the ground where he hits his head on the stone floor and gets knocked out.

The next morning, after Rikava awakes, Tran tells Rikava to leave his house and never come back, whereupon Rikava proceeds to travel the two-day journey to the Drogen tribe where he is received as a hero. At the same time, word gets back to the Empress that Rikava has betrayed her by selling weapons to the Drogens, and is now living with and training them. When the Empress hears of this duplicity, she quickly sends two assassins to the Drogen tribe to capture Rikava. He is captured, brought back to the Empress and during the torturing that preceded his death, he falsely tells the Empress that Tran had been knowingly making the weapons and selling them to the Drogen tribe all along.

Of course Tran didn't know that Rikava had been selling his weapons to the Drogen tribe but it was too late. Suti begged the Empress to spare Tran, but the Empress was adamant and Tran was hanged in the public square along with Rikava.

Chapter 6 The Scribe

I must have spent a thousand years being born and reborn in this small village at the junction of two roads, in the northwest sector of Wiomia Province. Mostly I was born as a man, sometimes a landowner, sometimes as that same landowner's slave, but really nothing much happened, which is probably why I kept going back there, afraid to explore, afraid to embrace new experiences, comfortable in the power structures that gave me safety. But a revolution was brewing in the land.

One day General TenTu came marching up the valley towards this small little village at the base of the white mountain. He is securing the remote provinces for the new Emperor and wants to quarter his soldiers in this little town. Very soon after his arrival, the General decides to send a fast messenger to the capital to tell the Emperor what he has discovered on his journey.

Sang-Tu, the village scribe, is asked to send a message to the Emperor, but once he hears the message, he immediately realizes that the General intends to attack and capture the small rebel band living in the foothills near the village. This is where his friend Roki is training mercenaries in their preparation for a rebellion against the Emperor.

Not wanting his friend in danger, Sang-Tu arranges for a second courier to be sent to Roki's encampment informing Roki of the General's presence in the town, and the opportunity they have to assassinate him there. A plan takes shape, but the next day, when that moment comes, and Roki is able to get near the General, he can't actually thrust the knife and is himself immediately slain by the General's guard.

When Sang-Tu hears of this, he is distraught and stupidly tries to kill the General himself, but is immediately killed by one of the guards. General TenTu then routs the entire village, takes all the food, conscripts all the young men, kills all the sympathizers, even if they weren't sympathetic, and sets fire to the few buildings along the main road and marches out.

Chapter 7 Death by Fire

Tran-Win was there first, sitting on the bench watching the rock water not flowing. He was deep in thought. I was very quiet and surprised him. When he saw me, he looked for my eyes. I looked down, not able to look straight at him, wanting to but not able to. We were quiet for a long time and then he asked me if I would sit next to him on the oak bench.

Tran-Win's voice was poetic and lovely even while he wore the body armor of the General's son.

I said to him, "Beloved Tran-Win, our love cannot be. I am arranged to be given to Ran-Ho. You are of the warrior clan and a former enemy of my regent lord. This cannot be. We must say goodbye now and we shall never see each other's face again." I was trying as hard as I could to make this sound convincing. My heart was breaking as I spoke. I couldn't let him speak, mesmerize me with his voice, lest my will dissolve and I melt into his arms. I went on.

"Beloved Tran-Win. You must return to the northern Ghin province where your father, the noble lord, will marry you to the daughter of Jin-Tan. Your kingdom will be united, your life will be filled with children, grand children and great grand children. You will rule the Five Provinces and have a long life."

"No, San-Woo. I do not want that life. I want the life with you," he answered quickly.

"No Tran-Win, my most dear, you must not think those thoughts. We have met only in the fleeting moments of a spring day. You...."

"Hush. Speak no more of the future. Listen to the sound of the no-water over the rocks. It is the silence of our love." Tran-Win fell silent then. I became filled with deep and passionate feeling for him. I turned toward him, only now looking him in the eye, eye to eye, for the first time since we had met.

"I love you more than the earth loves the sky. I love you more than the water loves the rock," he whispered. I began to cry; the tears rolled from my cheek onto my collar. I saw the possible future: We would marry and have children. I would live in his noble house and- but no! this could not be- I turned away as the tears became thicker and my happiness and elation turned to sadness and pain.

"No! Tran-Win No! this cannot be! Let me go. Let me go" I sobbed as I got up from the oak bench along the great no-water river rock where the magenta grove had hidden us from view. Sobbing, I turned once more to look at Tran-Win, who I now knew as my true love but whose love I would never know. I turned and looked at him as he was looking at me and, from the eyes of the great warrior, came the soft tears of pain and regret. I knew I had hurt him far worse than the lance of the enemy.

"Beloved San-Woo" he said quietly as our gaze became locked. "I could search the seventeen heavens and not find one like you. Let me take you with me. I can not live without you!" he cried as he got down on his knee and bowed his head gently.

"Do not cry mighty Tran-Win. You must forget me," I lamely replied as I too bent down on my knees to face him. His head became erect. Our eyes became locked. Behind his eyes I saw the true Tran-Win, the great Warrior, my protector, my beloved. I saw that our destinies were linked eternally and there could be no escape from this. I knew then that his sacrifice would be even greater than mine. I might lose my home, my family but Tran-Win would lose a kingdom.

Somehow knowing my thoughts, he said, "Beloved San-Woo, I would sacrifice my kingdom, my life, nay, a hundred lives and a hundred kingdoms for the sake of your love."

Our eyes stayed locked on each other. He inched forward on his knees. I inched forward on my knees. Within moments we were embracing. Moments later our lips were locked in passion. We looked into each other's eyes and without speaking we both knew that we would sacrifice everything for the sake of this love, for the fulfillment of this passion: there was no going back.

Neither of us heard the sound of footsteps on the path.

"Get up! Get Up! Get up!" screamed Ran-Ho over and over again. "What are you doing? Get up!!"

We both rose up immediately. I thought Ran-Ho would strike at Tran-Win; his anger so full that his cheeks were red with rage. I was so ashamed. I looked away.

Tran-Win spoke next. "Ran-Ho, most respected sir…" he tried to say.

"Shut up you idiot! Shut up!" Ran-Ho screamed. "How dare you come to the house of my noble regent, to the garden of my noble regent and behave so improperly. How dare you?" His voice was lower now, but the rage was burning still.

"Humble sir, I am the son of the King of the Northern Province. I am the grandson of the King of the Western Mountain. Humble sir, I love San-Woo with all my heart and with all my soul. I will make her Queen of the Northern Province. I will take her as my beloved wife," Tran-Win spoke forcefully and passionately.

Ran-Ho was about to explode. "Beloved wife! You fool, don't you see that she will never be your beloved. She is the property of the noble regent and you are the enemy of the noble regent. He did not give her to you! In a thousand years he would never give her to you. You are a dirty soldier not fit even to walk in the noble regent's garden. Now begone and be lucky you are not thrown into the pit. Begone, I say, and come here no more."

I had to speak the truth. I knew that, being a female, my opinion would not matter, but I loved Tran-Win so much, I couldn't let this go on. I turned and spoke what was true.

"Father, I love Tran-Win and we want to be together. We have always been together. We did not accidentally meet in the garden of the no-water rock. I knew he was here and I sought him out. I have dreamt of Tran-Win since before I was a little child. He is the beloved of my dreams. I want to marry him." I had spoken the truth.

Moved with deep feeling, Tran-Win cried out "Beloved San-Woo. I too have dreamt of your lovely face since my first memory. I have been seeking you out in every village I go to. You are the reason for my travels from place to place, not the military alliances my father seeks out. Now I can stop my searching for I have found you," Tran-Win said boldly and ecstatically.

While they were speaking, Ran-Ho had moved behind the closest Magnolia tree and came out holding a burning torch which he pointed threateningly at Tran-Win. As he backed away away, Tran-Win tripped against the rock of the no-water and fell backwards. Ran-Ho went over to help Tran-Win but just as he reached him, a large branch of the Magnolia tree broke off and was about to fall on both of them. I jumped into its path, trying to deflect the force of the falling branch, but it fell harder and faster than I could manage. The tree itself had fallen against me and it pushed me against Ran-Ho and the three of us became pinned under the weight of the tree. As it was falling, the tree had wedged itself against the fountain in the river of the no water rock and became unmoveable. It had crushed the bones in my leg and I was pressed very tightly against Ran-Ho's back. He was pressed very tightly around the limp body of Tran-Win.

Suddenly, a great wall of flame erupted from the bridge of the no-water rock. The oil cans that were stored below the bridge, and that were used to light the candles on the path, had caught fire. Too quickly to count in time, the flames exploded up from the bridge and engulfed the Magnolia tree that surrounded us. Within seconds, the entire garden was aflame and the three of us were pinned under the large broken branch of the burning Magnolia.

The fire was so hot it began to burn the clothing on our bodies. The three of us were pinned down by the tree, unable to move as the fire continued to roar. We pushed and pushed. Tran, suddenly awake, began pushing with all his strength but was able to move the tree only slightly. He broke the rock of the no-water that we were being pinned against with the force of his own hand, but it was to no avail. The flames became hotter, more intense.

We died then. When they found our bodies, they said that the heat was so strong that it had fused the skin together. We were buried in one tomb. The tombstone they used was the rock of the no-water which Tran had cracked to try to get us out of the fire.

The noble regent replanted the garden with new Magnolia trees. My mother continued to live on the grounds of the noble regent. Trans' father retreated from his war in the Eastern Province. I was not born in China again after that last life. Nor, if I recall, were Roga or Tendo. What a mess.

Book 3
Arabia

Chapter 1 The Story of Radhu

Radhu's parents were traveling merchants, selling special cutting utensils from town to town along the trade routes through the sparsely populated Iridian Desert. Life was hard. His parents could barely get food enough for their six children let alone themselves. When Radhu was seven years old, he was traded to Lomas the Camel Skin Trader in exchange for a new set of tent skins for his family. Lomas could always use another young boy to clean up the camel shit and if he was good he could learn to skin the camels. And so in this way Radhu was brought up in the house of Lomas who adopted him as his own. Tomas had 4 daughters and no sons. A dozen years passed peacefully with Lomas a generally friendly and benevolent patriarch.

Lomas' second daughter, Salomar, was thin and beautiful, with long and elegant fingers. Whereas her sisters were happy to work with the camel skins- cleaning, drying, tanning and assembling them into garments and tent skins, Salomar, on the other hand, would paint the camel skins with camel blood and other dyes, transforming them into beautiful tent coverings sought after by the rich merchants who traveled the trade routes.

Radhu, when he was not taking care of the camels, loved watching her apply the layers of color and dye, loved watching her facial expressions when she was satisfied or, even more, when she was unsatisfied and she would move her upper lip slightly to the left. Or sometimes, when she would be exceptionally displeased, she would take the entire camel skin and throw it at the wall. He was quite content to sit and watch her, get the paints and brushes as she needed them, talk to her about nothing really important.

Maybe Lomas noticed the boy's attention to his daughter, maybe he didn't, but it did not matter if he had as Salomar was already promised to Abba, another artisan in town, who made the copper utensils then becoming very popular with the travelers. He would make a good husband for her and she would be well cared for.

So it was quite by surprise when, one day, he found Radhu and Salomar locked in each other's arms in the corner of the barn where his prized female camel had just given birth. Lomas saw immediately the passion in their embrace, as well as its impossibility. He stormed into the barn and forcefully separated them, hitting each of them on their head but especially brutalizing Radhu. He had to teach this boy a lesson and he swore to the boy that if he ever went near his daughter again much worse would happen.

But Radhu and Salomar had become lovers and their passion could not be thwarted or denied. They found every opportunity to sneak off, beyond the range Tomas would normally walk, and thus spent each extra moment in the others' arms. Lomas, by this time, had become suspicious and, needless to say, several months later he found the two of them together again. He had been drinking heavily and his anger got the best of him. He viciously beat Radhu into a bloody mess and told the boy to leave the house and never return or he would surely die the next time they met. He left Radhu in the forest, severely bloodied and battered, grabbed Salomar by the arm and dragged her away screaming.

And die he would have if Morastes and his tribal band of robbers had not been coming across that part of the high desert, traveling west, just one hour later. He found the battered and bloodied Radhu lying face down on the desert floor, breathing his last breath and in a moment of unrecognizable pity, Morastes decided to help the boy. Little did he know that this helpless near dead person would become the leader of a rebel group that would, one day, force him to give up his power sword. But today he rescued the boy and brought him into his band of robbers.

After Lomas sobered up, and realized what had happened, he became afraid that Salomar might be with child and so she was immediately wed to Abba. But there was no child and over the next few years Salomar settled into her life with Abba. She was a dutiful wife, but she thought often and with longing for Radhu, who she heard had survived his brutal beating and become a robber warlord in the Western Province. She bore no children to Abba who then proceeded to wed one girl after another in a vain and fruitless attempt to father children. Abba died suddenly one afternoon in the 12th year after they had wed. Abba's brother, who had inherited Abba's wealth and wives was attacked by bandits on the way to claim his inheritance and died of his wounds before reaching Abba's house. Suddenly, there was no one in charge. The world had suddenly and completely collapsed.

Abba's entire household was now easy prey to bandits and Salomar and the other wives were helpless and afraid. She had never forgotten Radhu and now thought longingly for him, seeing in her mind's eye that leaving Abba's old house and finding Radhu was what she had to do. And so in this way Salomar, disguised as a young boy, with several of her painted camel skins, joined up with a trade caravan heading West.

Radhu, during those 12 years of living in Morastes's bandit camp, had become quite skilled at stealing and robbing from the traveling caravans. He was smart, quick and learned the bandit skills easily. But there were tensions inside the bandit group. Morastes was not well liked and not all were loyal to him. The previous winter had been cold, food had become scarce and the young bandits wanted to get going, get moving, find some action, while the older Morastes decided to stay put, wait out the cold winter. There was talk in the group that maybe Morastes should yield his power sword to a younger man, someone who could lead the tribe more forcefully. The tensions had been building as the winter had gotten colder and darker.

While Radhi didn't overtly support the conspirators, he also did not oppose them. He was practical, a survivor, and logic ruled his actions more than loyalty or duty. One day a situation developed where he was forced to choose between the rebel group and Morastes. He saw that Morastes had no chance against the larger and younger rebel group and he knew that they were plotting to kill Morastes if he didn't yield power. He saw that it was necessary, in order to save the life of Morastes, to join forces with the young rebel group with the clear intention of saving Morastes' life. The rebels were very happy to get a traitor from the inner circle and they immediately selected him as their leader and the rebellion proceeded with renewed enthusiasm.

It was thus a very big surprise to Morastes that, one morning he found Radhu in front of a group of young bandits demanding that Morastes give his power sword to the man whose life he had once saved and whom he treated as his own son. Morastes swore up and down but his bluster was thwarted when Radhu, standing face to face and breath to breath with Morastes, took the Power Sword and became bandit leader.

He felt sorry for Morastes and spent the rest of his life dismayed that Morastes would never forgive him for the apparent betrayal. Two mornings later Morastes, his wives, children, and a small group of loyal soldiers left the encampment. They traveled 200 miles to the west into the Far'quin Valley where, over the next several years, they reestablished themselves as a feared and brutal bandit family that terrorized the trade routes throughout the valley and extracted protection money from the local population of villagers.

On one particular morning, as the Morastes bandit tribe brazenly attacked a small caravan going north on the trade road, they captured and took prisoner the beautiful Salomar.

Within days of the attack on the caravan and the capturing of Salomar, the local army, a small division of the Iridian High Command, became aware of the location of Morastes's hiding place. That night, they attacked the bandit tribe and all were taken prisoner by the Iridian king's local adjunct, a General Tedic.

General Tedic reviewed his new prisoners who were mostly old and haggard desert rats, with missing teeth and unclean nails. All except one- a young woman who called herself Salomar. This prisoner was young, had skin like silk, with long and wavy hair the color of the black sand. In Tedic's eyes, she was the most beautiful woman he had ever seen. True, he had not seen that many beautiful things, given the life he had lived, but still, this Salomar with long fingers that graced the air, with her full and luscious body, captivated General Tedic like no other woman.

He knew he could have just taken her, forced his will upon her or made a slave of her to satisfy his desires. And he was tempted. More than tempted, he was compelled to possess her. By the third night of her capture, he could think no other thought as he paced relentlessly inside his tent. His lieutenants began to ask what they could do for their General, what new war was he contemplating, but how could he tell them the truth, that there was this young prisoner who was possessing his thoughts.

He would dream of her at night, dreams of meandering rivers with small little trees along the side or he would see her playing with children in a large castle. There were no castles like that here in Western Iridia, Land of the Sweet Water. Was he losing his mind? Was this woman a demon sent by the gods in retribution for his life of savagery and immorality? His brain just kept thinking…and thinking. He pushed all these thoughts away. His will was very strong, but barely strong enough to stay focused on his army instead of his prisoner.

Eventually word reached Radhu that the Iridian commander had taken Morastes captive. It had been 12 years since the split in the bandit tribe but as long as 12 years were, they were not long enough to make Radhu forget his fierce devotion and loyalty to Morastes. Over those years, guilt and remorse had eaten away at him: maybe he should have done it differently, maybe he should have sided with Morastes and fought against the rebel group. But there were more of them, they were very angry and intent on seizing control at any cost, even killing Morastes if they had to. And anyone else who got in the way. He didn't feel like he had a choice.

Now, however, he was compelled to do something, take action of some kind. This compulsion, to honor his bond with Morastes after all those years, seemed futile at first but this compulsion grew each day, and now, after a few weeks, he felt like he didn't have a choice. After several more weeks of brooding, Radhu packed up his bandit camp, anxious to travel to the Western Province and rescue Morastes.

Radhu and his bandit tribe traveled to the Fa'arquin Valley disguised as a cult of religious seekers, on a journey to Mt Kundu. Surprisingly through these travels, Radhu began to acquire a small amount of notoriety, and became an increasingly famous shaman, dispensing prayers and blessings as he and his ragtag band of followers moved through the various towns and villages. By the time they reached the Fa'arquin Valley, 200 miles to the West, their arrival was greeted with gathering anticipation. Who was this half-blind shaman leading a band of ragtag followers? Very quickly they were inside the Fa'rquin Domoda, where General Tedic had his troops quartered. When the General heard about this itinerant band of holy men, he invited them to his compound so they could dispense prayers and blessings to his troops.

And so this is how, in this particular lifetime, destiny brought them together, like magnets.

Chapter 2 The Story of Tedic

Tedic had been born in a prison camp in the desert, several hundred miles to the North of Iridia This was the cold desert, barren with rock, broken with crevices and steep ravines. Many prisoners had found their final resting between the rocks hundreds of feet down. Not only prisoners but anyone who King Vartag did not like. It was indiscriminate. His mood was completely subject to random whim and, more often than not, his whim led to savagery.

Tedic's father was King Vartag's main lieutenant. His title was Varlu which roughly translated as Vartag's arms. Tedic's mother had been captured in a sweep through the Andahar province where the men were killed immediately, the boys conscripted, and the women kept for a little while to serve Vartag's army. The Varlu, of course, could pick any of the women and he picked Tedic's mother, the most beautiful of the princess daughters, and who was then barely of menses when the Varlu used her. Unluckily she became pregnant, gave birth to a boy baby, but bled to death during the birth. The Varlu decided to keep the little boy baby, raised him as one of his adopted sons and trained him as a soldier.

By the time he was ten, Tedic was already quite skilled with weapons and by the time he was twenty, horrified at the Vartag's lack of justice and indiscriminate killing of innocent people, became the leader of a rebel group that fought against the Vartag and the Varlu. But the Vartag's army was stronger and they easily defeated the rebels.

Certain he was in deep trouble, Tedic had to run. He stole the fastest horse, left at a gallop and rode for 3 days straight. The horse died and he stole another horse. When his food was gone, he stole food and ran. He knew he could never go back.

He rode through the ice, up mountain passes, down through valleys. He kept riding west, following the setting sun. He rode at night, stole at night and slept during the day, far away from people, from roads, from farms. Vartag had given up the chase long after they had found Tedic's horse tracks leading up to the 20,000 foot Kushija Pass- in the dead of winter. He and his soldiers turned around there and went back to their camp, satisfied and laughing.

Tedic fought hard for survival on the cold icy mountain. But it was too much, too impossible to cross through the Pass in the dead of winter. Near death, frozen and starving, he began fading in and out of consciousness and at one point just collapsed on the snow and passed out. Lost in his dying dream, the other side beckoning, he was suddenly woken by sharp pains in his ribcage. He thought he saw a red hot iron spear penetrating into the side of his frozen body. Suddenly very alert he became very afraid, jumped to his feet, and began running. No horse, no food, no weapons, almost no clothing. Just fear, desperation, and the instinct to survive.

And survive he did. When he came down the other side of the Kushija Pass, weak and near death, he stumbled into the Persian town of Malamar. To the few people he stumbled past, he must have looked like someone risen from the dead. No one had ever come down from Kushija in the Winter. Where did he come from? How had this man survived? Was he with the devil? He looked completely inhuman, with his face bloodied and his clothing in complete tatters. As Tedic stumbled his way to the town center, the tribal leader was called. He sent his soldiers and bodyguards to see what this was all about and what they found was a near-dead man, ragged, broken and starving, lying face down in the town center. They had to kick him to see if he was alive.

But he was alive, though just barely. The soldiers brought Tedic to the tribal leader who looked closely at the face of this stranger. Something about the fierceness and determination necessary to cross the mountain in the winter were signs of a great warrior and his army could always use another warrior. In this way, through luck or destiny, Tedic survived the mountain and was conscripted into the local Malamar army. He grew strong.

Tedic had been living in Malamar for 15 years when events started stirring in this little part of the world. A warlord from across the river was not willing to join forces with the rest of the local tribes to create a Greater Persia. The Persian community in the Eastern Province united and had set their sights on the Western Provinces. Tedic was sent to the East to establish a presence in the rebellious land.

And so, in this way, Tedic had wound up in the Fa'rquin Valley with a half-blind wandering desert rat in his compound, as well as the young goddess he wanted to possess more than anything he had ever possessed in his life.

Chapter 3 Back to the Story

General Tedic, while enjoying the camaraderie of the itinerant shaman, was really obsessed with the girl he kept locked up in one of the rooms in the Damoda. One day he told Radhu about her, how he wished she would come to him, how he didn't want to force himself on her, how she was different from all the other women he had met. Radhu, of course, had no idea that this was the Salomar of his childhood.

Slowly, over the next several weeks, as her fear subsided, Salomar began to actually like this General Tedic. One night, three weeks after her arrival at the Damoda as a prisoner, Salomar allowed Tedic into her bed. Her life changed quickly after this. No longer a captive, she was allowed to roam the Damoda, and especially the gardens. She could sit there all day and paint her camel skins.

One day, Tedic and Radhu were walking through the gardens when they came across Salomar sitting there. Tedic was very excited to show Salomar to Radhu and as they approached Tedic asked her to get up and say hello to his friend the shaman.

Radhu recognized her immediately but Salomar, eyes cast downward, did not immediately see who was standing next to Tedic. Even if she had seen his face she might not have recognized him: the desert had scarred him and he did not look the same. But then he spoke.

"Hello, my name is Radhu. You are even more beautiful than the good General said," he saw himself mumbling. This was not possible. This couldn't be happening. He must be dreaming…

Chapter 4 The Story of Salomar

The next day, while the General was off with his soldiers, Radhu went into the gardens to find Salomar. She knew he would be coming and she was waiting.

"Radhu," she began formally, "what brings you to this Damoda?"

"What brings me here?, what brings you here?. What happened to your husband, your father? How did you get here? What are you doing here? Where are your sisters? Are you Tedic's wife? His servant? His concubine? What are you doing here? …" Radhu went on rambling. He reached over to touch her.

"No, you have to be careful. The General has spies and if they see us being too friendly it will surely get back to him," she said quietly, painting the entire time despite the huge waves of emotion that was rolling through her.

"What are you doing here?" asked Radhu again. Salomar proceeded to tell him everything that had happened to her from the time Radhu was kicked out of the house including the death of Abba, his brother, running away, and her capture by Morastes and then Tedic. Radhu had known some of this from Tedic's own talk but hearing it from her lips sent a shaft of physical pain through his body.

After a few moments of difficult silence, Salomar said "You better leave now, go…leave…leave this Damoda and never come back. Tedic would kill you in a heartbeat if he thought you were any kind of threat to him. Go away…and don't come back."

The years in the desert had hardened him and he was not afraid. "I will not cower. I am not afraid. He might be a General but he is still only a man. I have fought many battles. I will not run away from this one. I will fight for you!"

"But what are you fighting for? Are you fighting for me, to take me away from here into the desert.? I'm not sure I want to go. I like it here. Tedic is a good man beneath the harsh exterior. No, I don't want to leave."

Radhu was beside himself. How could she refuse? "No, you will come with me. If I need to I will kill Tedic….Come with me now, we will escape this place, find the love that was stolen from us a long time ago."

Salomar couldn't believe what she was hearing. How could Radhu, deformed and hardened, possibly think that she, Salomar, would want to leave the Damoda, run away into the desert and spend the rest of her life running, hiding, hungry and dirty. It couldn't be more clear. For Radhu, likewise, it couldn't be more clear. He had traveled all this way and divine providence had placed Salomar right in front of him.

And what about Morastes? He had to rescue him as well. His plan took shape: kill Tedic, free Morastes, take Salomar and run like hell back to the Eastern mountains. He sent a message to Salomar to get ready.

That night, the General's staff came for Radhu who was unceremoniously hanged in the courtyard of the Damoda, his body thrown onto the bone rubble at the southern bone pit. But Radhu wasn't ready to leave and angrily hung around as a ghostlike vapor spoiling as much food in the Damoda storeroom as he could. Then, when he was finally ready to leave, having extracted as much revenge as possible, he couldn't find his way out of the storeroom. His little ghost spirit spun exhausted circles inside the walls of the storeroom, burning in a fire of hate and betrayal. He never would have found the Way out, and might have spent an eternity spinning in circles of suffering and despair, were it not for the massive evolutionary shift that was about to alter the entire fabric of reality.

Chapter 5 The Priest and the Priestess

Shekilah's story began at age 3, when the High Priest, Rohan, came to visit and extract favors from Shekilah's mother, whose husband was off to war in the King's Legion and who lived alone with the other women and children whose husbands were also off to war. When the High Priest met the little girl for the first time, he immediately recognized her psychic qualities, her powers- in potential, perhaps, but trainable. Yes, he thought, this one could be trained, could be very useful 15, 20, 25 years from now, when the current king would be old and feeble, when his sons would vie for power- what a splendid idea to have a young priestess like this at his side, helping direct the course of events, guaranteeing the ongoing power of the Priests and the Temples. Yes, she would become the High Priestess of all Egypt and she would be loyal only to him.

When she was 10, before her first menses, she was taken to the Temple at Luxor, trained in the mysteries and taught the secrets in potions and spells. She was cared for by the young women who cared for and cleaned the Temple but was taught by the Priests under the direction of the High Priest. The other young female novitiates were jealous of the special attention she received. She spent much of her time alone, often in the private gardens of the Temple Adjunct, not himself a Priest but more like the manager or administrator of the Luxor Temple. His name was Aradin and Shekilah felt protected by his presence and soothed and nurtured in his splendid garden.

Things went on for 12 years in this way. By the time of her final ordination at age 22, Shekilah was a beautiful and mysterious figure, gracefully walking through the Temple, cloaked in shimmering veils with splendid onyx and emerald jewelry hanging from her wrists and neckline. Her eyes were dark, her lips red with crimson ointment, her fingers delicate and long, She spoke with no one and spent all her time alone, in meditation, in ritualistic ceremony, silently walking through the Gardens or along the paths through the catacombs. She would leave a scented trail in her wake and her room, restricted to all, was always emitting perfume and incense at all different hours of the day or night. The years passed. One day, Rohan knocked on Shekilah's door just after the morning ritual. "Priestess," he bowed, "we must talk." His voice was edgy, afraid, uncertain. She sat there, mixing incense powders in small silver trays. "Yes", she said simply, "speak openly."

"I have seen," he continued, "that the time has come for the Great Transition in the Kingdom. The old king has lost his grasp on events. His sons smell blood and are ready to go to war with each other. Depending on who prevails, the entire Order of Priesthood is at risk. One son would do away with priests completely, slaughter us all. One son would allow us to stay with reduced power. One son is completely in our confidence and it is this one, the young Bakara, who we want as the next King." There was silence for several minutes.

"Rohan, you have been plotting these events ever since I have known you. You know I find your scheming distasteful and unworthy of the High Priest." Her harsh response was not new to Rohan. Shekilah, while beautiful and skilled in the arts of magic, lacked the correct respect when she spoke to him. But he knew, and she knew, that she had to do his bidding. "What do you want me to do?" she said finally, exasperated.

Undisturbed, Rohan stared into the distance for several moments, then replied directly. "Shekilah, you may not know this but the King had another son- a fourth heir- whose mother was a commoner, and after the birth of this illegitimate child, the mother and child were banished from the palace. The boy grew up in the province of Goram where, decades later, he became a powerful General and is now stationed in the Northern Province. The other priests and I are afraid that this General Tenen, once he becomes aware of the developing situation here, will bring his army into the Kingdom and install the first son of the King, an enemy of the priesthood, into the Royal chamber. This would be disastrous for us, and for you, my dear, and would be the end of everything."

High Priest Rohan had laid out the situation but hadn't told the whole story. That he was afraid that Tenen himself would rise to the throne, once his real ancestry became known. Tenen, Rohan knew, would take down the priesthood as quickly as possible, starting with the High Priest. It was Tenen who Rohan was afraid of.

Shekilah was quiet. There was more here than he was telling her: she saw that he was very afraid and the circumstances were more dire than he was revealing. Without any emotion, almost sympathetic, she asked "What do you want me to do?"

"I want you to go to the Northern Province, find this General Tenen and, in one way or another, make sure that he never steps foot in this kingdom. Kill him if you must but he must not come here to help the heir."

Despite her strong will and general dislike of Rohan, Shekilah was compelled to do what he asked. Deep down inside she felt close to Rohan, somehow loyal and protective, and despite a floating antagonism, she slowly began to see the necessity, even inevitability, of them working together to preserve the Priesthood. She saw that the young heir, with this Tenen supporting him, was a threat to a way of life that had existed for thousands of years.

Over the next week, as she prepared to leave on her mission, Rohan spent more and more time with her, explaining the necessity of his plan and the absolute necessity of its outcome. The king's young son happened to be sending a contingent of his loyal soldiers to the region where General Tenen was encamped with his men and, surreptitiously, Rohan was able to get passage for Shekilah disguised as one of the supply helpers.

There is not much in the akashic field of what happened to Shekilah after she found her way to General Tenen. She never returned to Rohan but the General finally did not invade. Bakara was coronated King the next spring. Rohan lived into old age as chief advisor to Bakara, but pining every day for his missing Priestess.

Notwithstanding his huge grasp on power, the one thing Rohan wanted more than power, could never be his.

Chapter 6 The Test of Roho

The desert sun was hot beyond belief and if you stayed in it too long your clothes would catch on fire. It was easy for the desert to consume you, easy for the sand to swallow you whole. Many novices had died, in distress, during the last part of the training: no water, no shelter, no food. Three days of burning hot sun, burning hot sand, burning hot thirst. The trick was not to lose your mind, or, even less, your common sense. If you learned the techniques taught by the priests, if you were practiced in these meditations, you could control your thoughts and feelings, you could go into the altered states necessary to control physical reality and endure the 3 days. Then when the moon became full you could walk the 3 leagues to the desert hut where the water was sitting in a specially prepared water skin. And, after that, receive full ordination into the priesthood at the next New Moon.

At the outset of the three day test, the priests would place a very exact and precisely potent amount of fracinite, an odorless, colorless poison with a high dissipation rate, into the water. The fracinite would slowly neutralize over three days and, after the three day period, the water would be perfectly harmless. But at any point prior to the three-day active state, the water was a very potent poison that would immediately render the drinker into a slithering babble of mucous and blood. Death was quick, even if it was ugly to watch. But no one was watching and only when the guards returned would they find either a lifeless corpse spitting blood or a naked almost insane person begging for food and water. Of course great care was taken in the preparation of the poisonous brew. For those that survived the test, the secrets of the Priesthood, and the Path of Power, were revealed.

Roho was very anxious about the test. His teacher, Tuturu, while very close and supportive of Roho, was also very harsh and critical. If

Roho succeeded then he would be taught the Greater Mysteries and one day become the Senior Priest. If Roho failed, which meant death, then Tuturu would have to train another novice in the Lesser Mysteries- probably the new female novitiate that Tuturu was giving so much special attention to the young priestess, Solia.

"I am ready." Roho declared to the priest escorts who had taken him to the desert hut at the edge of Sand Mountain. "Prepare the water skin and leave." Roho declared in a strong and powerful voice.

The escorts placed the water skin on the small table. They watched the sun move carefully across the sky and when its angle caused a specific shadow to appear on the far wall, offered the water cask to Roho who took one last long draft of the clean water. Then they carefully poured the flask of fracinite into the water cask, making sure to shake the last few powder specks into the water. The priest doing the pouring then showed the empty flask to the other priest, who acknowledged that it was empty. Roho quietly undressed and gave them his clothing, whereupon they quickly left the desert hut.

Roho then walked the 3 leagues up the sand mountain, turned around to face the setting sun and stood there- naked, alone, with no food or water in the middle of a remote portion of an inhospitable desert. The sun started setting, the wind picked up, sand whipped across his face stinging his raw skin, quickly embedding itself into his orifices and pores. The sun quickly set then and night began to fall on the desert. The wind dropped off after sunset but so did the temperature. Roho sat on the sand mountain with his knees in front of him, his arms around his knees, trying to contain as much of his body heat as possible. He began to breathe deeply, rhythmically, bringing lifeforce into his breath and bringing his breath into his vital organs, one organ at a time, In this way he passed the first night. From time to time he would doze off but wake up with a start when he found his body shivering.

The first several hours after the sun rose in the East, Roho was a little comfortable. He knew it would get hot and that these early morning hours were his best window for doing a little work, preparing for the cold night ahead. He slowly dug a body size depression into the sand, only a little deeper. There was no wind and the work went quickly. By the time the sun had risen into midday and the heat had built into a sweltering inferno, his little sand house was ready. He would use this to place his body in for the hottest portion of the day and cover himself with sand. It would be hot, but at least he would be protected from the sun. He sat there quietly for most of the first day, buried in the sand continuously, calming his mind, deepening his breathing, lowering his temperature. This is what he had practiced.

In this way Roho passed the first day: quiet, conserving energy. When the winds came in the evening, he stayed protected in his dugout house until the wind became so strong that it blew the sand away. When the temperature dropped he started walking in concentric circles around the windswept dugout, establishing a steady rhythm, kicking his legs high, breathing deeply. He measured his exhaled breaths and made sure his outbreaths were longer than his inbreaths. This would allow him to build up a heat reserve in the pluniery wheel which he could use in the later part of the night. Which he did.

And then, suddenly, it was morning. The second day was not as easy as the first. His dugout was destroyed in the night and he had not re-dug it. He found himself naked against the midday sun, with hot sweat evaporating instantly. Afraid he would dehydrate and go into shock, he tried burrowing into the hot sand, and that helped a little, but his internal temperature had already started rising and it was hard to stay in control of his mind. By midday his delirium was so great that he could not make out the difference between the sand and the sky. Then he imagined that the sand was water and he took a large handful into his mouth. By nightfall, on the verge of defeat and obliteration, he lay naked in the sand, passed out in his own vomit on the side of a small sandy mound.

But suddenly, he awoke with a rush. Something was stabbing at his ribcage and it forced him to get up and start running. It felt like something was pushing him, propelling him forward, away from defeat. Every time he tried to slow down, take a breath, the excruciating pain in his ribcage got worse. He must have run for six hours straight until he collapsed again. And so passed the second night.

By sunrise of the third day his mind was so completely disoriented that he could not tell the difference between the setting moon- which was actually one day shy of full- and the rising sun. The full rising sun appeared to him as if it were the full setting moon and he mistakenly thought it was already the full moon of the third day. Suddenly excited and hopeful, he picked himself up and crawled back to the hut at the edge of Sand Mountain, excited that he had passed the test and eagerly anticipated drinking the clean water. He thought he saw Solia and Tuturu beckoning him, offering him the water casket, smiling with approval. Yes, he thought to himself, I made it.

He proceeded to drink the still poisoned water and died within minutes from an exploding medulla. As his spirit was jumping out of the convulsing body, he thought he saw Solia and Tuturu embracing, and then laughing, but in the next mind moment Roho lost all 4 dimensional consciousness.

The next morning when he didn't return, the priests went to find him. They picked up his lifeless body from the desert hut, carried him 5 leagues to the boneyard and dropped him over the edge where he landed with a thud on top of a thick layer of bones. Within 6 hours the desert scavengers had consumed every molecule of flesh and sinew.

But Roho was long gone and far away, absorbed in a swirling vortex of superimposed energy fields, layered with matrices of sadness and suffering, hopelessness and decay, crying into the wilderness where no one was listening.

No one was listening.

Chapter 7 Judea: The Path

I always tried to find places in the desert to recover, to find my soul. In the silence, in the raw unrelenting heat, in the barren landscape, I could be alone with the pain, the huge disappointment and depression that overwhelmed my thoughts with unrelenting feelings of betrayal and disillusionment.

Whatever it was, the desert could absorb it, maybe help heal it.

The desert sun is the same in different deserts on different worlds: a relentless glaring brightness that assaults the tiny membranes on the cornea and overloads the neurons racing backward from the eye into the cortex. There is no time left over for self-pity. There is no time to think, no time to feel sorry for yourself.

Though organic life is everywhere in the universe, even on the waterless planets, it's no wonder so relatively few species actually live in the desert, at least compared to, say, the wet jungles, or the northern ocean coastlines. The unrelenting oppressive heat and light create an environment where the soul is naked- naked to the wind, naked to the sky, naked to the sand, naked to the air itself.

While of course one must wear clothing for protection- from the sun, wind and cold, no one is fooled by this human adaptation. No one. Nature scoffs at this human attempt to control her. One can perhaps live in the desert, even get born, have a life and die in the desert, but one is never fully at home here. One can never be fully settled and at ease.

For myself, I gravitated towards this empty space to escape the relentless assault on my emotions and feelings. I don't like the desert particularly, except for that one quality that makes the empty ambience completely worthwhile: no one lives there.

Except for the rare hermit or the isolated hermitage, few people come to the desert just for fun, or to hang out. I understand that changed somewhat in the middle days, when whole groups would vacation near the few water spots and run loud machines through the barren landscape. But these individuals would come and go; soon they would leave for good. The landowners and government caretakers said they needed to protect the desert from erosion. They said it played an important part in the overall ecology of the biosphere and whole sections of the desert became off limits. Except for the few that had been living there, the desert remained empty, just the way it always had been, and should be, from before we started counting time.

Passing into unconsciousness, not wanting to remember the cumulative assault on my soul thread, I went into the desert to lose myself, lose my individuality, try to forget the dark and stupid things I and my friends did to each other, over and over again, mercilessly. One lifetime after another, over and over again in a relentless assault on the mind and body, generating confusion and conflict from the edge of one star system to the other.

Even now, thousands of years later, I am moved to tears when I think about it, how much pain and suffering I created and allowed. My beloveds and soul mates. Too much. I just want to go to sleep.

Interlogue

Ladro, looking quite robust and gratified, is pointing to the largest, most central pipe feeding into the Generator. Aung, looking a bit weathered, is only half listening to Ladro. Another part of him is clearly distracted.

Ladro was talking rapidly. "Look Aung, just look at the fuel line. It stretches for billions of light years in every direction. The Creator was sure right. Adding that sentient stuff to the death energy sure made a difference. So much raw energy being directed into the Generator. These sentients are amazing. They're just so compulsive and obsessive. The whole entropy problem is solved. Creation will never run down; it will run forever. The Creator said this would work. It's fantastic. This is the secret which will sustain the Creation. I don't have to stress any more about my calculations and things like "the coexpansion coefficient" or "the delayed ionic proton parameters." I just have to work the mechanical side, make sure the turbines are greased- if you know what I mean." Ladro was clearly happy.

Aung tried to listen, though he continued to be distracted. One could only imagine what his celestial eyes were seeing. "Yes Ladro, the turbines will run forever but at what cost? Is the continuity of Creation worth the cumulative cost? The massive underlayment of pain and suffering, the oceans of despair and unhappiness- the millions and billions of individual suffering minds and bodies, the huge waves of destruction and disgust, the pathos of individuals, of communities, of nations and whole planets" Aung was palpitating and distraught. "I don't like it!"

Ladro, agitated, responded quickly. "Yes, yes it is worth the cost. Creation would have dissolved long ago back into the primal non-existence. Remember that? You were there. Right? This way, you get an ongoing sustainable Creation: recycling Death and now this Sentient suffering into Cosmic Fuel. Brilliant! And anyway, I am just doing my job..."

"Ladro, I'm only saying what's obvious: that the amount of suffering arising out of the sentient mindfield pathology is too much! It's just too much!! This can't be the only way to maintain the cosmic continuum," Aung answered as his attention began to wander off.

Just then Aung sees, in the great distance, millions and millions of sentient beings mentally calling for help, crying and wailing in confusion.

Some macro level tragedy must have occurred in one of the hundred billion galaxies. Aung gives Ladro a piercing look, begins to vibrate and shimmer and then disappears. Minutes later, when he returns, his garments are in disarray and his eyes are swollen and red. Ladro is in the same position as before, sitting in front of the transwarp computer array, having not moved at all. While he's glad to see Aung again, he is unsympathetic to Aung's inner turmoil. New generators have grown in size and intensity. Large pulses of light shoot out from the central matrix; additional substations appear out of nowhere.

Aung continues with the same pleading tone of voice. "That was just unbelievably horrible, Ladro. This can't go on. Fuel for creation or no, the will of the Creator or no, there has to be another way. So much death and destruction, so many broken bodies, broken spirits; so much anguish and despair. I don't care if creation has to run down and stop. It's not worth the price. Between the hunger and the violence, between the greed, the fear, the hatred, the destruction, between the broken minds and the broken bodies it doesn't add up. It's too much! I have to find a way to stop this madness, this unrelenting pressure for fear and intolerance, for selfishness, for hatred and revenge, for unending suffering and despair!"

They'd obviously had this conversation before. Ladro had his answer ready. "No, Aung. There is no other way. We can't stop it. This is what happened when the Creator embedded the sentient code into the Creation. He made it so that we use their discontent, their continual agitation, their fear, their anger and hatred, their incessant dissatisfaction, in short, the encapsulated micro ions of their mental and emotional suffering and discontent to keep this Generator in operation. Remember the task He gave me: maintain the Creation at all costs, keep it going, do not let the entropy run the system down. He said He had made a promise to someone or something. You seemed to know what He was talking about."

Aung shook his head. It was true what Ladro was saying. Aung knew that He had promised Her that He would sustain the Creation for Her, for Her Dance. He replied back to Ladro. "But there's got to be another way to keep this machine going- this can't be the only way to generate more fuel, relying on tormented and dissatisfied little sentients- this can't be the only possible way for keeping the engines stoked. In the hundred billion megagalaxies, in the infinite potential of the cosmic mind, in the aeons of multi-dimensional time, in our experience in possibility and impossibility, surely we can find a better way!"

Ladro, having heard this plea a thousand times, was ready with his quick answer: "- Oh Aung we tried and tried. Remember, it's a systemic thing. He hard wired it this way. He did it on purpose... He...."

Aung cut him off. He was getting angry and was starting to lose it. "You don't know that. Maybe it was just the easy way out. Besides I think you secretly enjoy all that unconscious suffering, you're a closet masochist- you're evil and cruel." Aung began sputtering. "You're a nihilist and misogynist. You're..."

Just then, Aung's eyes began to go out of focus as he gazed off into the distance. Once again, he began to shimmer and vibrate and disappeared quickly. Ladro sat there a long time looking off into the distance and when he returned his attention to the Generator he seemed quite pleased. More pipes had appeared feeding into it and the amount of smoke coming from its chimney pipe had also increased. Ladro folded his arms and began to walk toward the main entrance to the building when Aung appeared, visibly shaken and distraught.

He continued the conversation where he left off, in the same tone of voice. "The amount of destruction was unbelievable. Two worlds collided and 30 billion sentient beings became delinked from their bodies at once. They were undeveloped, some still living in their caves and were not prepared for the collision of worlds. Their cries will echo through the nine levels of existence until the end of time. Their loved ones, their caves, their little houses, their ancestral graves, their hopes and dreams, the little children trying to find their mothers at the end, the great walls of water drowning whole populations, the mountains sinking back into the ground, the explosions ripping people's bodies apart, the..."

Ladro couldn't stand it anymore. "Stop it! Stop it! You indulge in all this sentimental feeling. These beings are dead, dissolved, they are decentralized loci fragments of electrons and neutrons. The whole sum and quota of their last fearful mind moments are becoming fuel for sustaining Creation, for the continuity of Creation itself. Look Aung!! Look how the fires burn! Look how many more eons of existence have been generated! You call it tragic but it is great, according to the laws of God Almighty, for His purpose. Stop feeling so bad for what has to be, for the inevitability of this agitated disharmony with existence and then the necessity of death. At least we are using this energy for good purposes, for sustaining Creation. Those worlds would have collided anyway. I didn't make that happen. And nothing you or I could have done could have stopped it!!"

"You're a monster Ladro. You have no compassion, no place in your narrow selfish mind to cry even one tear, one tear?" Just then, Aung broke down completely, sobbing and sobbing. Within moments, however, his head picked up and the characteristic glaze came over his eyes. Silently, he shimmered and disappeared. Ladro, alone again, continued inspecting the generators. At least he had to make absolutely sure that the equipment was in perfect shape and no energy was lost inside the mechanics of the machinery. It had to work with perfect efficiency.

After a short while Aung returned again, visibly beaten and shaken up. His clothes were uncharacteristically ragged and torn, but an unexpected sparkle in his eye told Ladro to pay attention, that Aung had some new cockamamie idea on how to stop him from doing his job managing the cosmic generator.

"I've been thinking Ladro," Aung began once he had settled down. "Maybe you're right. Insofar as the Creator has made death, and now also discontent and dissatisfaction, intrinsic to sentient existence itself- and apparently there is nothing we can do to stop it- then maybe you're right. That's it and that's the way things are."

Aung wasn't finished but Ladro could already see where this was going. He didn't say anything as Aung went on. "Maybe what I find unacceptable is that these beings, while sentient and more or less a little bit aware, have no choice in the matter, they have no say in their own participation as fodder for some weird cosmic engine that they don't know anything about to begin with. They are being led to slaughter, as little more than fuel nuggets for the Cosmic Power Supply and they don't know it. They are put up as sacrifice without any agreement or acknowledgement on their part. There is something wrong with this picture. There's no freedom here, no compassion, no honesty. The sentients are in a prison, making fuel rods for the Corporation and they didn't really do anything wrong to begin with. It's unworthy of the Creator's grace."

Ladro was getting really tired of Aung's sentimentality. Nervously, he fidgeted with some dials and switches on his main control board and a huge blast of yellow foul smelling smoke discharged from the nearest smokestack. Aung cast a stern look at Ladro.

"Listen to me, Ladro. There's something wrong with this picture. To those creatures that are not sentient, which is most of Creation, the basic discontent and the awareness of pain, decay and death is not present. While they experience change and decay on their own level, they don't really suffer. It's only the sentient beings, with awareness of themselves and others and who are cognizant of their own death and the death of everyone around them, who suffer. It's only these sentients, whose intense myopic dissatisfaction rises to this peak fuel level quality, who suffer. What bothers me the most is that these sentient beings are given no choice, that they are born into a miserable life of constant petty dissatisfaction only to satisfy our own need, or the need of the Creator as we understand it."

Ladro really wasn't listening. but Aung continued anyway.

"Here's what I'm saying Ladro. What if the sentients had the choice to use their own personal discontent- which we see comes automatically with their sentience- and which ongoing fragmented ions would ordinarily be used by the Engine- but through their choosing to break free from that default prison sentence they can, through their personal efforts, get released to live as a free and liberated consciousness."

"What if the pervasive malcontent itself became the tool to help the sentients jump out of the hellish pool of conflict and arrogance they find themselves in? What if they could escape from the narrow sentient prison which was unfairly thrust upon them without their knowledge or consent?"

Ladro was getting agitated. What the fuck was Aung talking about! "Get to the point Aung, I can't wait all day for another convoluted ass backwards justification for your stupid and childish sentimentality."

Unfazed, Aung continued. "I think I've figured out a way to use any sentient efforts to wake up, any effort to get free from their pervasive malcontent- from the chemistry engendered by the effort itself - to generate small quarks of fuel-ready ion proton plasma," he said, as he moved over to Ladro's main computer terminal. Needless to say, Ladro wasn't pleased that someone was messing with his stuff. Smoke spewed out one of the secondary pipes. The neon calculator in Ladro's hand started buzzing and pulsing.

"Ladro, just listen…" as Ladro reluctantly put the calculator down on the table in front of him, "…so here's my idea," Aung began, "if we look at these equations at the third sub-nucleonic tier," he said, as Ladro leaned over his shoulder, defensive and uptight, "we can increase the bo-son speed here, at the proton boson jump," he said pointing to the 6D isometrics, holographed on the primary monitor, "then, as a consequence, way over here at the sentient level, each individualized effort of will on the part of the sentients to wake up, to interrupt the normal waking sleep, generates these very very tiny ionic pre-photons. See, look at this Ladro," Aung said ecstatically. Aung was screaming now, pointing to a small spot in the middle of nowhere. "Look! Look Ladro!"

But Ladro was only looking for mistakes that Aung might have made, ready to attack and ridicule.

"Aung," Ladro quickly replied, frustration rising in his voice, "re-member we tried that with the ProCreative project. Where we asked the sentients to participate in the Creation using their natural creative intel-ligence and all we got was more conflict and destruction as they became so infatuated with their power to control the world that they made a huge mess of those worlds where we tried it. Those worlds were destroyed and it almost caused a total meltdown in the baseline matrix. Surely you remember how much extra work you had to do."

"But this is different. We would not be asking them to help co-cre-ate the world. That was giving the sentients too much power, too much importance. We expected too much. That was our fault; we didn't think it through. This is different. It's not getting the sentients to co-create their worlds, just that we open the possibility for individual sentient beings, who so chose, to transform their own consciousness in order to be free from a lifetimes of habitual suffering. Give the sentients a choice. That's all I'm saying."

Still acting disinterested, an exasperated Ladro replied: "Aung.... Aung, we tried everything. These little creatures, spitting hatred and self-ishness with every other breath, are not designed for this kind of personal freedom. The Creator built it this way. You saw the design blueprints- you even signed off on them....remember?" Aung didn't answer. "You can't be messing with the basic structural grid. That's not our job. And how do you expect to do that anyway? Change the way the Creator set it up... are you crazy?"

Aung continued. "No, no, Ladro, you haven't been listening. Noth-ing changes. No, all I'm asking is that the sentients have a choice, that their participation as fuel rods for the cosmic engine be a choice, not a prison sentence," declared Aung, "and now that I've figured out a way to do it with no loss of Engine fuel, everybody wins!"

Ladro couldn't believe what he was hearing . "You mean that the sentient beings could stop becoming fuel for the Generator if they wanted to? You can't really mean that. Aung, you're an idiot! It's contrary to the Creator's intention. That's completely ridiculous and I will have no part of it. The Creator entrusted me to do this job and I will not be sidetracked by a wimp, clever though you may be. You have to toughen up Aung. These are just silly little creature things who come and go in the blinking of an eye. They are of no consequence. Why do you care so much? The whole thing seems to be working fine, why do you have to mess with it?"

That was a fair question, Aung realized. After all, it was the Creator who set this whole thing in motion. Why should he care so much? His job was only to help soothe and direct the sentient beings in their transition away from their biological life form. So what if they wailed and cried. So what if little children lost their mothers and fathers in floods or war or famine or neglect. So what if they could never really be happy for more than a few moments before the underlying fabric of their discontent resurfaced. So what.

But Aung replied back to Ladro. "His intention is only that the Creation proceed. I don't think He particularly wants mass suffering. It just defaulted that way. I'm only asking that we try another way, that we use the sub-quark bosonic energy generated when the sentients make even tiny efforts to transform themselves, increase their awareness, and try to get out of their unconscious suffering. When they figure out the state of ignorance they are in, and then try to change that, they begin to make efforts to wake up, And it's that effort, that energy, that we can use as additional fuel. Ladro, Check the calculus."

Although this seemed like another one of Aung's stupid dea for Ladro, it was at least intriguing. Ladro was still sure it would not work and would be relegated to the dump alongside the ProCreative project and other futile attempts to make Aung feel better. But he was obligated to look at it and at least take it a little seriously.

"Let me think for a minute, Aung." Ladro then walked off toward a secure room in the Generator building, sat down at the desk, pulled out a second neon calculator and performed some complicated algorhtythmic subroutines. Moments later he was back talking to Aung.

"If you want to do this I'm willing to give it a try. My numbers show me that, even if those redirected ionic pre-protons don't work, and we lose those sentients, the maximum net decrease in generator fuel is a small fraction of a transrational microton. Acceptable risk. No big deal. Also, I predict that you will find that not many of these beings would be willing to give up all their deluded ideas about themselves and the world in order to get transformed.. They become so mesmerized and hypnotized by the pleasures of terrestrial existence and so numbed to their own and others' suffering that they're not even thinking about it. They don't want a way out. They're not going anywhere Aung. You are way too sensitive. Grow up!"

Aung wasn't sure. "You're probably right Ladro, some will, some won't. It's just the idea that the beings who are trapped in the sentience and who might want a way out of their personal discontent can get out. If the other sentients want to stay inside the causal wheel, continue to live in habitual darkness, then they can do that. At least there will be choice. I think that's all I'm after here. Just that these sentients might have a choice."

Actually there was no risk for Ladro. As time proceeded, many more worlds were evolving and sentient beings were becoming prolific in all the known universes. There were so many fragmented, disconnected ion particle streams fueling the Generator that, what the hell, so what if a few of them opted out. No big deal. Anyway, Ladro thought, it would never work. Might as well give Aung this small concession. Poor old guy, he had too much work as it was, trying to comfort the billions and trillions of beings as they wound their way through birth and death. "It had to be tough." thought Ladro, uncharacteristically sympathetic.

"OK Aung. Let's try it," remarked Ladro. suddenly feeling very generous. Just then, that glazed and pained look crosses Aung's face as he shimmers and disappears. Ladro, left alone, begins thinking to himself. "Yes Aung, yes. This could be fun. I didn't say I was going to make it easy. Let me see- if I push here and pull here, if I stretch this network matrix and put some grease here—there---now that should do it."

The cosmic furnace belched out enormous amounts of a white-blue smoke. Small secondary pipelines began to emerge from the main control tower. Additional dials and levers appeared on Ladro's control board.

Off in the distance, the Creator was smiling. His lips were moving, and He was swaying back and forth as if engaged in an animated conversation. He knew that this was the beginning of the end, that sooner now, rather than later, His outbreath would complete itself and, before His inbreath could begin, Creation would be stopped for a few long moments. He smiled. He was counting the days.

Book 4

The Saints

When Aung returned he found Ladro tinkering with the various dials and switches on the control panel.. To Aung's amazement, Ladro had constructed a trans-warp communication device and was messaging the far flung cosmic overlords about the massive reorganizing of the Cosmic Engine that was being planned.

The first thing Aung noticed, when he entered the conference room through the edge of the parabolic inversion that Ladro had created just for this occasion, was the large glass central table. It was round and made of a combination of purified photonic titanium and ordinary Athenian glass. The titanium was quark sized and embedded in the glass. The glass edge itself was polished, which allowed the reflective quality of the photonic alloy to permeate the entire table. The table glowed with its own internal luminescence.

Around the table were set twelve chairs, each made of a different material with its own unique shape and color. More than a thousand earth years later, a great terrestrial King would try to duplicate this configuration, trying to advance the cause of enlightenment in his native land. Surrounding this central table were three continuous and concentric rings of tables, supporting various pieces of equipment- most of which looked like futuristic communication devices made of a 12th dimensional shiny alloy. There were wires, or what seemed to be wires, extending in 8 directions. Unlike the central luminous table, these rings of concentric tables were plain, not self-illuminating, and all the chairs were the same style- very basic and functional except for the lighted headrest. It was obvious to the casual observer that these concentric table rings were where the work got done. The stripped down functionality of these ring tables contrasted sharply with the other-worldly beauty of the central table.

Slowly the space began to fill up. First, the outside concentric table rings began to populate with dozens of technicians managing the enormous communications array. Huge multi-directional spotlights illuminated the work area as the technicians connected vast laser and holographic arrays into the main Engine. Every so often a shimmer would vibrate through the complex machinery and Ladro would shout at someone or turn a specific switch or, more rarely, smile with a look of satisfaction. Aung stood off in the distance, watching in amazement.

After a short while the technicians completed the last assemblies of the holographic arrays and everything appeared ready. Silence descended on the triple ring as the center table began to pulsate. The internal light became brighter. Some of the techies were tinkering with some final adjustments but most sat silent, expectant, apprehensive.

And then… a cloaked figure appeared off in the distant darkness, seeming to come from the edge of the dark matter itself, and slowly moved towards the center table. Flashes of hydrogen lightning pulsed randomly from the being's cloak. The entire triple ring became totally silent as the cloaked figure drew closer. No face was evident behind the hooded cloak; only a robed being, seeming very old, slightly built, in dark colors with its face completely hidden by the cloak's hood. This nameless Rishi, mythologized on most terrestrial worlds as the Ancient of Days, or on some as The Zarathustra, or on others as Sanat Kumara, had maintained a continuous interactive physical link with the seven physical planes of existence since the dawn of Creation. No one had ever met him or had ever talked to him; no one knew where he came from or what his role was in the matter of universal functioning. What everyone did know was that he was the original author of what the Gaia people called the Rig Veda, the basic foundational spiritual engineering textbook which would be translated into more than 75 million languages and become the core spiritual teaching on 100 million worlds. Because it originated in the Sapta Sindhu, the Land of the Seven Rivers, everyone assumed the Ancient One abided there, notwithstanding that none had ever been 'there'. Aung and Ladro, both visibly in awe, bowed gracefully in the Ancient One's direction as he proceeded to sit down in his non-descript chair. As he folded his hands on the table and removed his hood, sparks of purple light shown out from his eyes. Stillness pervaded everything.

Within moments, the patriarch known on Gaia as Abraham materialized out of thin air, or thin space, as it were. It began with a slight crackling sound in the background ether, which grew into a larger and larger deep bass hum, similar to the hum which accompanied the Rishi, but deeper, more physically pounding. Then, suddenly, he was there. He was not only not wearing robes and did not have a long grey beard but he appeared young, wore an illuminated lycra space suit with electronic gadgetry affixed to his wrists and neck, with leather boots that reached up to his thigh. His head was shaven except for a small round pile of golden blonde hair spiked on the top of his head. His long ears were pierced with multiple holographic ringlets shining brightly. He appeared to be jittery, even impatient. As he sat down he began tapping out erratic rhythms on the Table with his hands. After several minutes, the central photonic table as well as the concentric ring tables began to pulsate. The beat became louder, more defined. Everyone was shaking as the deep bass sound permeated everything. Abraham continued to beat the table with his hands. Some of the hi-tech equipment on the concentric ring tables began to spark. The beat became louder as more equipment sparked; some pieces began to smoke. Still, Abraham kept increasing the tempo, pounding harder on the photonic table. The rhythm became more and more complex and at one point it morphed from the rhythmic drum beat to a universal shattering crescendo: surely this was how the Creator made the Creation: He had Abraham do it with his drum. And then it stopped. Just like that, the drum beating stopped. Everything stopped. The absolute stillness and incomprehensible silence that followed was ear-splitting. It was the sound of the inside of everything, the sound of the empty space between the electrons. Everyone except the Ancient Rishi had to cover their ears. Time passed and slowly the silence abated as the background sound of the Engine began to rise up. Abraham moved in his chair, crossing one leg over the next as he winked to the Rishi. Whether the Rishi winked back, none could say.

After a few moments the entire space around the Central Table began to shimmer again. Waves of liquid light, coming from beyond the concentric rings, began to cascade and eddy onto the titanium table. The liquid light waves merged and melded into each other, its fluid, joyful light suffused with deep sacred resonance. Slowly, meticulously, various forms within the wave singularity began to emerge. They appeared to be different female forms- old, young, with wings, without wings. Some had long grey hair with layers of folded garments cascading off their bodies while others had short spiked hair, wore tight fitting clothing studded with jewels. Slowly a composite being began to emerge in the middle of this whirling liquid light lava, mesmerizing all who watched. She was a beautiful being, wearing a long dress made of desert sand with amethyst thread. Her hair was long and dark with grey at the sides. Her eyes were a radiant dark, her skin luminous, her lips crimson. Everyone there, including the Ancient Rishi, was humbled by her transcendent Beauty as she took her seat at the other end of the Great Table. She sat there, divine love radiating from every pore of her body, enrapturing and holding all who looked upon her. They called her Mary.

With the Great Table anchored on 3 sides by the Rishi, Abraham and Mary, the other Board Members began to filter in, albeit with less fanfare. Lao Tse walked over to where Miriam was sitting, bowed deeply and sat down. He carefully placed his folded hands on the table top and sat completely still whereupon Mamia reached over and placed her hand on his. Several moments passed as the two auric energy fields visibly merged and then separated. Lao Tse smiled broadly as a few words passed between them. They continued to hold hands and concentrated their attention on the empty chair next to the Rishi.

Slowly, dimly in the background, the celestial choir began chanting. The volume increased slowly and then, in the next moment, everything and everyone became silent. Even the hum of Ladro's engine became still. Suddenly, somehow, as though from nowhere, from the emptiness itself, sitting in a golden chair was the great Maitraya Buddha, perfectly serene and resplendent in royal robes made of ruby and emerald. For several long moments a deep, sacred and profound stillness pervaded the entire assembly as well as the empty and dark space between. Then, slowly, his holy celestial light became so bright that all those present had to shield their eyes. The great beings seated at the table brought their hands together and bowed their heads as Maitraya sat silent, radiant and illumined. A great and powerful light permeated the closest hundred million galaxies.

Directly across the table, Socrates sat pensively, watching the pantheon of spiritual beings gather. Patanjali, with pen and notebook in hand, sat down next to Lao Tse. He was the designated scribe for this meeting and had agreed to take notes. Then, suddenly, the room became silent again as the assembled group awaited the arrival of the next celestial being. Everyone knew that the Solar Logos, Christ himself, was due to arrive at any moment. They waited and waited. Time had stopped. After what seemed like forever, the assembled beings began to breathe deeply and in synchronicity. After several long breaths, and at the point where the combined inbreath switched to the outbreath, just in that moment, the space between the empty protons began to vibrate. Thousands of forms and faces began to morph into one another and slowly a composite being began to emerge from the formlessness. And then there stood… the Christ, the Singularity, the manifest form of the Creator Himself. All the divine beings acknowledged His presence. Even the ancient Rishi bowed his head before the Son of God.

Just as Christ was getting himself situated in a simple wooden chair, the wind began to stir and the air began to crackle with bird song as the Feathered Serpent, Quexacaotl, sat down in the chair next to Mary. Last to join the table was the great Saint Mohamet, who, with dagger in one hand and rose flower in the other, sat down quickly and forcefully next to the enormous presence of Christ.

When everyone had been seated and calmed down, Maya stood up and began to sing the Invocation. Celestial light and sound danced across the table. Threads of gossamer began to entwine themselves with the misty airstream of her breathing as various great beings began to coalesce into form and crystallize -- some partially manifesting as wispy air alive with multi colored wings, some fierce and battle weary, some benevolent, some beautiful, some bruised and beaten. In the constantly shifting panorama of Miriam's Invocation - the goddesses Ishtar, Isis, Uzza, Aphrodite, Durga, Shakti, Saraswati, Lilith , Sophia, Hera, Mami Wata and Kali appeared in a spiraling orgy of compassion and love.

When this symphony of love and form had subsided, Mary stood silent for a moment and then brought the concentrated focus of all the great cosmic beings onto a single point in the middle of the center table. And in the center of that focused micro point of energy, she compelled the underlying protons to expand with great force saturating the multitude of worlds, blessing all of Creation.

When the World Mother was done, the Center Table became quiet. The triple ring had almost melted from the heat of these Great Teachers and the Mother's powerful invocation. Slowly the lights began to flicker, techies began turning micro dials and the triple ring began to rev up. Within moments the great world teachers were engaged in a cacophony of conversation, rising in crescendo then becoming suddenly quiet and then rising again to a feverish pitch and then again becoming silent.

The Council of Nine and their various incarnations quickly morphed into a cosmic symposium. At the main plenary session Ladro and Aung both keynoted. They described their differences on the subject of species evolution, emphasizing their respective roles as determined by the Creator. They elucidated the reforms to the sentient envelope they had engineered and Aung went on about how an 'evolving' sentience could become an intrinsic and self-perpetuating attribute of existence, both feeding energy into the Engine, while maintaining a dignity for life. Ladro, of course, emphasized what he thought was the idiocy and stupidity of the 'selfish robot creatures,' as he called them, and the futility of their achieving any higher consciousness, and that, as the basic fuel for the cosmic generator, it was their biologic death that served an important and significant purpose.

Aung spoke eloquently about compassion, but also emphasizing that he thought only a rare, negligible number of sentients would seize the opportunity to become transformed. and thus were unthreatening to the larger mission of sustaining creation. At the conclusion of their remarks, everyone agreed to a new common imperative: allow for sentient beings the possibility to transform their existing pervasive discontent into a higher level of vibration, becoming free from automatic suffering.

The plenary ended and the delegates and their staff began working in subgroups. Various tracks had become identified but the biggest challenge was integrating the work of previous avatars, previous visitations from Lord Buddha and Jesus, for example, and figuring out how, if sentience hadn't yet existed prior to this conclave, what were these cosmic beings doing thousands of years before? It was decided that the core matrix of linear time needed to be adjusted .037 degrees to accommodate these prior visits and have them show up as a parsed-destiny causative factor. Hundreds of powerful acolytes, in deep trance, proceeded to move the River of Causation just that amount.

The technicians at the ringed tables were moving faster than possible, recording and translating the multiple conversations. Patanjili was dutifully taking notes, his hand flying across the holographic keypad almost faster than the speed of light. Other break-out group were discussing the innumerable ways that sentients could develop themselves, could individuate, grow their soul bodies, become transformed and wake up from the dream. After the timeline adjustments, that was the biggest challenge- figuring out how the sentients could become aware of their dreaming and instilling a desire in them to wake from the dream.

Other sessions were devoted to discussing the efficacy of different techniques relative to the various planets and star systems, identifying which species, which bodily composition, which conditioned environments lent itself to which path, which technique, which access to the consciousness of liberation. This part was extremely difficult given the huge varieties of beings in the 100 billion galaxies. Some beings lived on planets made of aether, had only aetheric bodies; some planets were on fire; some planets were only water and the sentient beings had only water bodies, and mind floated through the liquid molecules in modalities completely different, say, from terrestrial bodies. Needless to say, it was enormously complicated to create a road map to liberation that could apply to these huge differences in the mind/body relationship on all the different worlds. At one point, Abraham became angry and shouted at the celestial beings to slow down lest they miss some important detail, forget about some obscure form of sentience on an impossible world. They had to be careful.

In other groups, they were discussing which of the archangelic beings would be responsible for which sections of the universe. They decided that Christ would manage the 108 Archangels. Lord Buddha was put in charge of all the non-manifest planes of existence. And so on. Each celestial being took ownership of a specific function, specializing on a specific level of spiritual progress. Slowly a plan began to emerge. Patanjali took copious notes which after the meeting could be translated into various texts and disseminated into various sentient cultures as needed.

The three ringed tables buzzed with activity. Vast arrays of lights and pulsing photonic sound resonances permeated the entire work area. Emergent streams of ribbon like DNA shot out from the sub panels and disappeared into the 100 billion galaxies. The entire universe was about to be transformed: transformed from a blind and ignorant sentient consciousness into an emergent liberated possibility.

And then it was done. The celestial beings sat down, silent and... still. To the untrained eye it appeared as though nothing was happening, but in that profound silence Aung saw the future being modeled, rich with possibility and anchored in Divine Love. Divine Love, which had always permeated the neuronic underpinning of Creation, below the surface of immanent awareness, would now become available to the sentient mind in their ordinary waking state. If the sentients wanted to remain unconscious, closed to the higher possibilities, then their struggle energy and their death energy would be reabsorbed by the Engine. So be it. If, on the other hand, they wanted to escape from the Necessity of ignorance and suffering, and instead manifest Love and Joy through their soul stream, then they could create that reality and cease to become merely recycled fuel cells for the cosmic fire.

It was done. The universal fabric of sentient existence had become alive with new possibilities. Inside the neurosphere. the possibility of Freedom and Liberation was now endemic in the fabric of existence.

The Council of Nine reassembled at the Center Table. The triple ring continued to buzz with activity. After a long silence, Mary stood up and as she drew her breath in, the myriad forms of her deity withdrew from her breath filaments. She stood there, unadorned, with simple garments, eyes sparkling with laser light. Silently, she raised her hands, extending her palms upward. Then, in the blink of an eye, the cosmic overlords were gone.

The Central Table stayed illumined for several more moments and then it too disappeared. The workers at the concentric ring tables took a little longer to tie up the loose ends but then, moments later, they disappeared also. Ladro got back to work. A far-away look crossed Aung's eyes as he shimmered and disappeared.

The Creator, watching from the distance, smiled.

Book 5

Eurasia

Chapter 1 Yaweh

After Abraham and the Ancient of Days came back from their long walk, Abraham connected up with Moses and gave him the difficult task of bringing God, the Creator Himself, into a living and accessible form, and into the lives of sentient beings, in order to help them in their quest for salvation and transformation.

It was a miracle itself that the Ancient of Days could convince the Creator to get involved in this personal way. It was anticipated that His direct participation with the newly upgraded sentient mindstream would help them take a big leap into the new possibility that was opening up for them: helping the sentients acquire an aspiration for something other than their sleepwalk and self-gratification.

But where to get started? What stories to embed in the historic mindstream to function as bedrock and foundation for the divine revelation? Working the various timelines, Abraham's team studied all the possible historical futures, making sure to take into their central calculation how recent sentient evolution actually was in historical time. For most three-dimensional beings, survival and fear were still the basis of, and most common relationship they had with, the natural and supernatural world in which they found themselves. Fear of the unknown, fear of the night, fear of death, fear of their enemies, fear of the natural world around them. This was the key: use that fear to jumpstart the new sentient evolution.

Linking to this deep DNA spiral ganglia as a starting point, Abraham reorganized historical events in order to bring the Creator's physical presence into the historical timeline at the precise evolutionary moment-in-time necessary to maximize His third dimensional impact. He directed Moses to introduce to the sentients a fearsome God, One who would resonate with their survival based fear and their need for a Great Father to watch over them and protect them from an unfriendly world.

Moses' plan was a find a tribe of sentient beings that he could isolate for a generation while he overshadowed their DNA with the new possibility of freedom and liberation, and inculcate their culture with the profound religious faith necessary for the Realization of God as a personal Immanence. And there, in Egypt, a tribe of semites, building pyramids for the Pharoah Ramesses II, became the focus for Abraham's terrestrial experiment, as he revisioned the Israelite destiny to include the Creator's visitation at Mt Sanai. With help from the future Prophets, he was able to establish Jehovah as a living presence among those sons of Jacob, one of many starting points for the insemination and saturation of God's perceivable Presence in the minds and lives of sentient beings across the universe.

Over the next few thousand years, as cosmic alignments shifted and sentient consciousness matured, the fearsome God of the desert morphed into a God of compassion and forgiveness. The actual presence and participation of God the Creator in the envelope of sentient consciousness was very powerful and the possibility of transformation through religious faith and devotion to God accelerated quickly. His Presence allowed the sentients, at least those that had come to Him, to move beyond their suffering and into a progressively illumined, awake and aware consciousness.

Inside this powerful Divine Light, and over the next cycle of our incarnated experience, the three of us began to come to terms with the awful and terrible things we had done to each other, to ourselves, to others. And now, notwithstanding the active Presence of the Creator in our lives, and despite the Grace it has brought, our selfish, painful and bloodied trail was not so easily dislodged from the karmic substream.

Chapter 2 Theopolis

Theron was born into a rich Roman family in northern Judea, not so much by accident, but because there was a premium on Jewish peasant bodies during that time and he had to take whatever he could find. There was rumor that Christ, the Solar Logo, was going to manifest in a terrestrial body on the planet Earth as the peasant Jesus. All manner of incarnated and disincarnated beings wanted to be near that singularity, to be alive during that mega event. Of course the entire population of Judea at that time was very small and so you could imagine the demand on little Judean bodies. Maybe because of his good karma or maybe he just got lucky, but Theron was born as the son of a well-to-do Roman captain stationed at the northwest corner of the Galilea basin. The Captain was charged with the protection of the booming trade routes throughout that region and which were vital to Rome. This was the trade that flowed overland from the East, put on boats in the Mediterranean ports and freighted over to Rome.

Theron's early life was uneventful. Protected and pampered by his grandmother, who lived with them in the great house, he was brought up completely segregated from the general Judean population. He attended school with other Roman children, spoke only in his native language, dressed only in contemporary Roman clothing and looked with contempt upon the dirty conquered masses. They lacked manners and seemed particularly loud and brutish. From time to time he travelled to Rome with his family where he learned the finer details of modern Roman living.

The arrogance that naturally comes with this type of superior life was shattered when, soon after his twelfth birthday, his mother took sick with the coughing sickness while his father had been travelling to India. His grandmother had become too old to maintain the house and so he was sent to live with his father's sister back in Rome. Although the house in Rome was beautiful, he felt like a total stranger. There were no other kids his age and his aunt, being very involved with Roman society, was never there. One night this party, the next night that party. The years passed as Theron completed school and entered military service.

Through his family's contacts he was awarded a position with the regional Engineering Group and began working on hydrology projects in the mountains surrounding Rome. He had developed important new concepts in water delivery systems which brought him to the attention of the General in charge of Aqueducts in the far away land of Judea. And so, twenty years after he was forced to leave Judea he returned as the commander of a construction battalion, previously commissioned in 57 B.C. by Julius Caesar, to build aqueducts throughout the conquered lands.

Theron arrived by boat in the northern port city of Tisla and went immediately to the Captain in charge, introduced himself and presented his papers. The Captain had known Theron's father quite well and so Theron was given the best quarters, the best horse and the best men. His commission was to survey the entire country, identify all water sources, develop efficient and effective ways of carrying the water where it was needed and, most importantly, protect the Roman supply from sabotage and terrorism.

Three days after his arrival in Judea, Theron left with a contingent of Roman soldiers on the Northbound Road leading up the Jordan River into Galilee and thence into the mountains of Syria. Over the next several weeks they plotted the water tables, identified the wells, measured the river's depth and flow rate and otherwise became fully immersed in their project.

One night, when the moon was full in the second month after the summer equinox, in the 4th year of the reign of Augustus, Theron was taking a walk in the late evening along the edge of the Galilee basin. He often went out alone, despite warnings from the Roman soldiers that it was unsafe. He was admiring the stars and the reflection of the moon on the still water. He did not hear anyone behind him and so it came as a complete surprise the sudden and severe blow to his head. He fell on to a pointed boulder, was knocked into unconsciousness and slowly bled to death, his blood flowing into the Galilee basin.

It wasn't his death that was remarkable, nor the deaths of the eight peasants subsequently rounded up by the Roman soldiers and put to death in retaliation. As he was dying, in the moments after his heart had stopped beating, in the moments after the soul had been forcefully ejected from the lifeless corpse, in the few moments it took finally to break the silver cord, a great hand had scooped down, grabbed him, and brought him face to face with the Cosmic Being. Christ's laser-like eyes penetrated into the core thread of his spirit and altered the distances between the electrons in his nuclear body.

After several long moments, the direct gaze of the Christ receded and Theron realized he was no longer in a transfixed state. Actually, when he took stock of his whereabouts, he found he was quite alive, sitting in his room at the Church of the Star in the Greek fishing village of Theopolis. He was already quite old, with long white hair falling around his shoulders. He had been praying and performing prostrations when all of a sudden he remembered his last days as a Roman soldier in the Galilee and especially what had happened after his death. Tears began flowing and landed in large drops on his magenta robe.

The people of the church and the village where he performed religious service noted that some great change had come over their old priest. His eyes, always bright, had become luminous. His affection for the community had become transcendent. He lived a very long life and when he died at the age of 103, his body did not decay for 1 month. People came from all over the countryside to see the glowing aura of the old deceased priest. Pictures were drawn and wood carvings were made and painted. Three thousand years later, the story is still told to the children of the village, about the great saint that had lived there. Of course life has gone on and the value placed on these things is not quite the same.

Theron was born and reborn into the same Greek Orthodox faith for 750 years. I guess when you find something you like you stick with it. If you read the *Early Fathers of the Philokalia* you can find Theron's writings under the name of Gregory. To this day, thousands of years later, despite multiple complicated lifestreams, when my faith wavers even a little, I reread those writings, and the intimacy with God that Theron experienced becomes very alive and powerful. I am sustained by it.

Chapter 3 Southern France

The church bells always rang at sunrise. Sometimes the animals would start chattering earlier, but mostly they waited for the church bells. Standing on the turret of the church, waiting for the first ray of sun to show itself over the eastern mountain, vigilant and alert, Brother Timothy always rang the morning bells. He would begin watching for the first ray starting an hour earlier, to make sure he didn't miss it. Day in and day out for seventeen years now he had plotted the seasonal movement of the sun on the interior of the church turret and so knew precisely where the sun's first ray would fall. But today Brother Timothy hoped the Sun wouldn't rise.

Yesterday, Sister Simone died.

Brother Timothy was so stricken with grief that he did not want to ring the bells. To announce what? That his beloved had died? It seemed like the world had ended and the sun should not rise.

It was his fault she had died so miserably, so dishonorably, alone in the forest, shunned by her community. They had loved each other since they were children, growing up in the same village upriver from the local church. Perhaps because of that young lust and its sinful nature, they both chose the religious life and, after ten years of living in separate monasteries, and by fate alone, wound up in the same parish in southern France.

Their passion could not be denied and within a short time they had revealed themselves before Jesus as sinners. And they suffered for their sins with extensive penance through self-torture and self-mortification. Even with long fasts, blood drawing, needles and fire, their love could not be denied and despite their inner torment of guilt and shame, they would meet in secret and consummate that love.

Father Roland was senior priest and received confession from Brother Timothy. Over the years of this ongoing sin, Father Roland had commanded Timothy to harsher and harsher penance and mortification to atone for his sins. Father Roland was challenged by the dual role of silent witness to confession and the unexpected pleasure he received in the suffering of Brother Timothy. He was not without compassion for the suffering of others, but it was different with Brother Timothy. Unmercifully, Father Roland thought that the younger Priest had deserved whatever punishment he got and so gave Timothy harsher and harsher penances, and in a twisted way drew more and more pleasure in Timothy's suffering.

And then… Sister Simone died.

Timothy's guilt, sadness and extreme distress was too much, even for the strong and valiant Timothy. But it was the pain from knowing that he would never see her again, never touch her beautiful hand or her cheek that was the most difficult. There just had not been enough time to love her. And now there never could be.

Timothy lifted the bell hammer as high as he could and began to cry out to God. Searing and gut wrenching he cried out. "Forgive us O Lord!

Forgive my beloved Simone!" he cried and lamented and cried more. And the Creator stood there, next to him, and cried with him. "She has brought you to Me," He whispered. And they cried and held each other.

When the first ray of sunrise began to peak over the horizon, Timothy hit the bell so hard it broke into a thousand pieces. He swore he saw Simone smiling at him before he collapsed on the floor of the Bell Tower and passed into unconsciousness.

Chapter 4 The Elephant and the Shaman

I only remember one moment in this life, when I was standing alongside the Great Highway that connected Banglador with Kiamesh as a large caravan of a rich merchant was passing. Dozens of elephants and wagons, hundreds of soldiers with bright armor and pointed swords traveled with the caravan. As was customary, all the travelers highway had stepped aside to let the caravan and entourage pass. All except one, an old man, who was obviously deaf and blind and appeared completely oblivious to the surroundings. He seemed so old and decrepit that it was impossible that he could even be walking on the road at all.

When the people near him realized that the soldiers were almost upon him, they tried to push him aside but he steadfastly refused to budge. Stopped in the center of the road, the old man turned and stood directly in the immediate path of the lead elephant. The soldiers moved quickly in front of the elephant and were nearly on the old man when the strangest thing happened.

The elephant, a large and beautifully adorned creature, stood up on its two rear legs. The elephant's master was nearly thrown off but somehow managed to stay attached to the elephant bridle. Then the elephant made a very loud sound which bellowed from the elephant's mouth. It was completely and without a doubt the loudest sound I have ever heard. Oh, I had heard the sound of avalanches, the sound of a thousand trumpets in the King's guard. I had heard the waterfall in the Kioshi Mountains. I had heard the thunder of the monsoons and the crash of the tidal wave. But nothing compared to the sound of this one elephant as it stood in front of this one deaf and blind man.

The soldiers stopped in their track. All the people on the side of the road stopped. Many held their hands over their ears. Little children began crying. I swear the trees on the side of the road started shaking. The roar of the elephant must have lasted only a few seconds but it seemed like forever. The whole world stopped in those moments. No one could take a breath. Even the sun ceased its movement across the sky.

It was in that surreal time moment while the elephant roared, in that impossible second when the world stopped in front of that deaf and blind old man, that I had this huge flash of awareness. Right there, in that moment something deep and profound vibrated up into my pineal gland. It felt like I had been shaken awake from a dream. Everything was the same, except it was real, not dreamlike. It was only a moment, to be sure, but beginning at that moment my entire life changed and everything was different.

When the elephant was finished roaring, he lowered himself back onto its four legs. The bystanders and witnesses thought that the elephant would surely charge at the old man. Then the second most extraordinary thing happened. Within moments of the elephant lowering itself back down, it bent its two front legs and began to bow down to the old man. It bent itself at the knee and lowered its head to the ground. All those who witnessed this extraordinary event had the same experience: the great and most noble elephant was prostrating himself to the deaf and blind old man.

Everyone was completely transfixed. And then the third and final thing happened that, in other circumstances, would have been extraordinary but, in the current context, seemed almost believable. The old man took his walking stick and waved it at the elephant in a gesture which told the elephant to rise- which it gracefully did. And that was it. The old man then turned around and proceeded down the trail and got lost in the crowds that had originally stepped aside to let the rich merchant's caravan proceed. At first people made a pathway for him, but quickly the throng of the mass movement of people and animals re-engulfed the road. And he was gone.

Chapter 5 Act of Truth

It was in my 34th rainy season as a monk at the hermitage near the town of Kofung in the district of North Mektilla. One day a wandering monk arrived from a monastery in the north and asked to stay the rainy season, which was just then upon us. His name was Tien Tien and this is the story he told.

He told us that he was born in the Thopal Protectorate, just east of the capital. As a young boy he was very sickly, and his family was very poor. Each year the parasitic diseases would devour him and year after year he would lay deathly ill for several months, then recover slightly, then get sick again. His body would never be strong and he would never work the rice fields, never go to school, probably never get married. He was taken care of by his family and especially, of course, his mother, and also his youngest brother who seemed particularly sensitive to Tien-Tien's deteriorated condition. The years passed this way. When his parents died, were it not for the goodness and compassion of his brother Saburo, he would have been left to rot in the swollen river. His brother took him in and he became part of that family.

His brother's wife was a very pious woman and helped take care of the local temple and many monks would come to his brother's house on their alms rounds. One day, several months after Tien Tien moved in, still sick and unable to get up from the bed, his brother's wife asked the senior monk to come to the house and pray for the young man.

And this is what happened: The six monks began chanting at sundown and chanted continuously, nonstop, for twelve hours. They were naming and chanting the Ten Doors of Perfection, gaining access to the sublime states of consciousness wherein lie extraordinary powers and knowledge.

At sunrise, after the twelve hours of continuous chanting, the senior monk, an aged and venerable holy man, announced he was going to perform a specific ritual, originally performed during the lifetime of the Buddha, called the Act of Truth. Everyone became quiet. After an hour of silence and a final clang of the bowl, the old monk declared that though he was rigid in his discipline and had been practicing the Ten Perfections conscientiously his entire life, he shamefully admitted that he never lost his desire for life, for the urge and passion of life. As he was saying it, you could see in his face the agony of this revelation, the deep humiliation he felt at realizing, and owning, his own weakness, his own lack of discipline and readiness after a lifetime of work and struggle.

Time stopped. The monks sat there with their eyes closed, then began another chant which only lasted several minutes, whereupon they got up, bowed goodbye to all of us, and quickly left. Although Tien-Ten's twisted body was still racked with fever, somehow everything was different.

As Tien Tien told the story to us many years later, while the old monk was reciting the Act of Truth, a great Force had somehow come into his body and he started shaking. Slightly at first, then harder and harder, he found himself pounding on the earthen floor of the hut. As his family watched, the pounding became louder and louder, in exact synchronicity with the rhythm of the second chant, louder and harder, screaming at God, breaking through the thick wall of karma, healing someplace dark and hidden.

Incredibly, over the next several days, Tien Tien's body began to heal, and he began to feel completely like a new person, with increasing energy. His body, though still emaciated from malnutrition, was pulsing with vitality. It was a miracle. At the next New Moon, Tien Tien went to the monastery, was ordained into the Sacred Order, dedicating his life to the Power of Truth that had miraculously healed him. And that's what he did: he taught us the way to transform ourselves and the world by speaking and living the Truth.

After the rainy season Tien Tien left the hermitage and we never saw him again.

Chapter 6 In the Bar

I didn't always get it right, that's for sure.

Rawlins is sitting in the pub on Newlander Square in the late afternoon. He had already drunk too much and was more than a little tipsy when Lorianne walked through the door. She was the local seamstress, slightly large around the mid-section, who enjoyed her pint every day just at this time. Lorianne sat at a table near the back of the pub with

Grantham and Peter and they talked and joked and slapped each other on the back.

Rawlins was feeling particularly unhappy this day. His wife, Sally-ann, was at home, alone in her wheelchair, knitting another shirt for him which he didn't need or want or even like. "What a useless person she was, stuck in a wheelchair, unable to do anything but knit knit knit," he thought to himself over and over again. And then I have to leave the pub early to take care of her." He was getting angry just thinking about it. "I don't want to take care of her. No children, no pleasure, nothing except knit knit knit."

And so on this particular day, wrapped in delusion and self-importance, ignoring the voice of compassion and tolerance, Rawlins didn't leave the pub early but instead got drunk with Lorianne on the upstairs bed, and left Sallyann alone for too long. Something happened and she died that night, alone and in pain, curled up on the floor in a fetal position.

Chapter 7 Delphi

Delphi was a great city in its day, a crossroad of the Aegean culture, midway between Athens and Byzantium. Aristo joined us in this life and was born first, married and became the father of 12 children. He was a local artisan and made the pottery for the community. Fragments of his work were actually discovered in the late 19th century during an excavation of the Temple to Adonis just outside the town walls. I had planned to meet him in his old age when I would marry one of his daughters. But things don't always turn out the way we expect.

I was born along the side of the main military road several days travel just north of Delphi. I met Theron there 15 years later when I was conscripted into the army and he was my immediate superior. We became friends and after our completion of military service we set out together to find our fortune. Theron had cleverly engineered a spring-type mechanism that enabled the traditional bow to throw its arrow faster and harder than before. Seeking our fortune, Theron and I set out for Byzantium where we thought we could find a good business selling this new weapon to the Persian soldiers stationed there.

So we set out on our journey to become wealthy, find our wives and conquer the world. Theron's unspoken goal, unknown to either of us at that time, was for us to meet up with Sonia, marry her and become patriarch of a large family.

And that is how, on one mild and sunny afternoon, somewhere on the road to Byzantium, we walked into the central square of a small fishing village. Amazingly, hundreds of years later, I can remember these images in exact detail as if this happened yesterday. The center of the town consisted of a few stone buildings alongside the main north-south road and was surrounded by trees and animal pens. It was right across from a small lake. People and animals were in constant motion, getting water, washing their clothing and utensils, sitting around small fires, playing musical instruments, dancing and singing. I can even now recollect the smell of fire infused with roasting lamb. Theron and I were captivated by the sounds and smells, by the people, by the energy. And the women. There were so many beautiful women! Slowly we made our way to the stone building where a clever person had put large wooden tables and benches outside and where other townspeople were seated drinking the local brew from large wooden goblets.

Theron and I sat down and looked around. We had been talking for only a few minutes when a young woman came up to us and asked if we wanted something to drink or eat. Theron pointed to the other table and asked for the same as they were drinking and several minutes later she brought us the two goblets.

She said her name was Sonia. She asked where we were going and we told her our plan to go to Byzantium and sell the new weapon. We all hit it off right away, almost like old friends, and she sat down with us and we talked and laughed and drank more goblets. After several happy hours I fell stupidly asleep at the table.

I kind of vaguely remember being carried from the bar and brought somewhere. When I woke up I was lying on a soft pad on a floor in a room I didn't recognize. The room was empty but I could hear Theron's booming voice from the next room. I got up, shook the sleep from my eyes and went in. Sitting at a table were Theron, Sonia and, as I learned, Aristo and several of his children. They were all delighted to see me up and about and Theron came over and gave me a big hug.

I didn't see it then but the madness and obsession of my Tendo/ Sarah story had somehow become unhooked and I was able to be truly happy with them being happy with each other. I don't know how that happened but it did.

Theron and Sonia were soon married. Theron kept refining his invention and was able to establish himself as a master blacksmith where he sold his redesigned weapon to the constant stream of travelers that passed through. I stayed as Aristo's apprentice, had my own family, and we all lived peacefully and that was a very fun life. We never made it to Byzantium.

Chapter 8 Europe 1880

At his oldest sister's wedding, when Rudolfo was fourteen years old, in the grand and ornate Church of the Holy Cross at the top of the Hill in San Bernadino, there were so many beautiful girls that Rudolfo thought he had gone to heaven. His sister had so many friends and each one of them was beautiful but none was more beautiful than Santiana. He had always loved Santiana, as far back as he could remember. As a young boy he would play off in the corner of the garden while his sister and her friends would talk and laugh. Santiana was usually there and Rudolfo had a difficult time not just staring at her. But she was several years older than he and it was beyond his wildest imagination that she would even notice him.

Rudolfo came of age soon thereafter and was trained in the family business, a trading company that bought and sold locally grown grapes and olives to the burgeoning markets in the south. Rudolfo learned the business well and had a good knack for keeping records, managing the trade documents and the various invoices and payments.

When his father and uncle were killed in an avalanche in the northern mountains, Rudolfo inherited the family business which he proceeded to expand into a sizeable import/export company. He became an established member of the community and was considered a 'good catch' by the local matchmakers. Rudolfo, however, had found none could compare to his primal memory of Santiana in the garden. Everyone was inadequate.

Consequently, Rudolfo lived mostly alone and isolated and, over time, developed a preference for it. What need did he have of marriage, of love, of the burden of family? So what if it was his destiny to stay a hermit. In this way the years marched forward and Rudolfo became more and more isolated and alone, eccentric in his isolation and aloneness.

He died alone and, sadly, never knew that Santiana, years and miles away, had the same longings, the same ongoing thoughts and feelings about Rudolfo. She had noticed him staring at her from the corner of the garden and always made sure she looked good when she went to visit. She loved Rudolfo but could never say that to anyone.

Her marriage was unhappy and she dreamt often of running away, finding Rudolfo and proclaiming her secretly guarded love for him. When she became a widow and had means to travel, she often looked out over her garden wall, where she had painted magical scenery of faraway places, and kept imagining Rudolfo sitting in the garden watching her.

Sadly, Santiana died alone also.

Chapter 9 Forgiveness

I wish I could just repeat this same life over and over again and not bother with all the other memories and experiences. When the direct gaze of the Christ receded, Terris realized that he was no longer in the transfixed state. Actually, when he took stock of his whereabouts, he found he was quite alive. sitting in his little cell at the Monastery of the Star in the Greek village of Theopolis. He was already quite old, with long white hair falling around his shoulders. He had been praying and meditating when all of a sudden he remembered his last days as a Roman soldier in the Galilee and his role in the Crucifixion. Tears began flowing and landed in large drops on his magenta robe.

The people of the monastery and the village where he performed religious service noted that some great change had come over their old priest. His eyes, always bright, had become luminous. His affection for the community, always rich, had become transcendent. He lived a very long life and when he died at the age of 103, his body did not decay for 1 month. People came from all over the countryside to see the glowing aura of the old deceased priest. Pictures were drawn and wood carvings were made and painted. Two thousand years later, the story is still told to the children of the village.

I have forgiven Tendo and he has forgiven me. The pain and suffering we caused each other through the ages is just a memory now: the memory of our blindness, our selfishness, our selfedness. Now, when we are born in the same time and the same place, we find each other without fail and we laugh at our eons of struggles and forgetfulness. Sometimes when Sita is also born at the same time and we all arrange to meet in physical bodies it gets a little complicated, but we work it out. I remember especially a wonderful life we had in Russia before the revolutions, when the czars still controlled everything. Life went on then and people were happy and sad just as they are now. Sita was born first and she was our older sister. Tendo and I were her baby brothers whom she adored and protected.

We lived in s small village in the foothills of the Ural Mountains. Our father was in the service of the Prince, though I'm not quite sure what he did. Sometimes he would be gone for long periods of time, almost as though he was gone off to war, but since there was peace in the land that could not have been true. We grew up together, then moved out into the world separately as we got married and had families of our own. Tendo moved far away and we never saw him again in that life. Sita and I remained near each other but we had our own families and did not spend much time together.

Curiously, Tendo and I died on the same day and Sita several days later. When we met in the afterworld we rejoiced in being back together and clung so tightly to each other it reminded us of that last life in China at the no-water rock. We laughed and laughed at the silly drama we created, the way we took ourselves so seriously. Naively, as future lives would show, we thought we had it worked out, that it would be easier from then on.

Maybe out-of-body it was easier, but once back in the body, the difficulties of human existence, of being alive, of unresolved karmic threads, was very present. And, of course, in the process of being born, we would have forgotten the deeper reality as we plunged again and again into earthly life.

Book 6

America

Chapter 1 Two Money Stories

First Story: Booksellers

Timothy was sitting looking out the living room window. He gazed over the rolling hills, green from the autumn rain after a parched and arid summer. He was thinking about the imminent arrival, any minute now, of his business partner, Raphael, returning from Italy after a month long business trip.

Raphael and Timothy had been friends and business partners for twelve years. They were in the business of buying old books from estate sales, bookstores and collectors. They bought books at a below market price and then would sell them online at a fair market value.

Sometimes they might get lucky and find a rare collectors' item at a low price. In this way, Raphael and Timothy kept themselves busy in the rare book business, were able to travel, stay at nice places, eat good food and generally enjoy a prosperous- even bon vivant- lifestyle.

In addition to having a general knowledge of rare books, Raphael was particularly knowledgeable about early European Paleolithic cave art, specifically the La Marche cave at Lussac-les-Chateaux in southern France. He was networked into the academic and collector world, constantly negotiating for this museum or that collector. Rafael was a sharp businessman and good negotiator and would often say, in jest of course: "I really 'stole' that book."

Timothy, on the other hand, was very savvy in marketing and knew the private collectors and auction houses where rare books fetched a high price.

They had met at an art auction in Los Angeles where they found themselves bidding against each other for pieces that were in the personal art collection of Hilary Vanderbilt, deceased second wife of the famous William Henry Vanderbilt. The collection was in pristine condition and included an actual section of the cave wall from the La Marche cave taken apart and shipped in large crates to California. Very quickly the bidding got out of hand and both Raphael and Timothy had to withdraw from the bidding. On the way out of the auction hall they happened to be next to each other and started up a conversation. One thing led to the next and within the year they were partnering in the rare book business.

Watching the clouds move across the sky, Timothy began to plan how he would market and sell the new collection that Raphael was bringing back with him from the trip. It would be very easy to sell, now that the internet had become the primary marketplace for buyers and sellers across the world. Buyers were everywhere now, not only the obscure rare book collector, but libraries, museums, dot com collectors and random individuals who would never have had access to rare books before but were suddenly eager to purchase rare books. Timothy was thinking about the language and strategy to use inside eBay as well as marketing to his dedicated customer list. He used what he called the "the default eBay strategy" to compel his customers to pay higher prices by saying, at the end of any discussion "or else I'll just have to put it on eBay." And after his customers lost the books they had wanted a few times, they had come around and were quite happy paying higher prices, never letting it get to market.

Suddenly, his cell phone rang. Raphael was at the airport and Linda was picking him up. She was waiting for him as he exited the terminal walkway. Linda was as enticing and seductive as ever, and Raphael marveled again how lucky he was to be with her. She dressed very conservatively in dark earth colors accenting her dark blonde hair. Only her red scarf gave away her fashion-conscious persona. Once inside the car, their conversation immediately turned to "the book".

"Where's the book, I want to see it," she began. "I'm so excited, this is what we've been waiting for. Our chance to…"

Raphael interrupted her "I don't know. I don't feel good about it, something's not right…I don't know…"

"What do you mean 'something's not right'. You found the book. You studied the ancient texts, you tracked it down, you did the whole thing. Why does Timothy have to reap the reward? It was your knowledge of those stupid caves that led you to the book. You did it. We don't need Timothy," exclaimed Linda aggressively.

"I don't know," he said again, obviously conflicted about what she was saying, "I've been working with him for a dozen years. It's almost like he's my family. I can't just lie to him, rip him off."

Linda responded, her voice rising in pitch with more emotion, "What about our family? What about you and me? I don't want to live so meagerly any more, and now we have this chance to really cash in. And besides, it's not like you're stealing anything that belongs to him. You made the discovery, you bought it with your own money, our money. Just don't even tell him. There are enough other books to sell. He won't even know."

Raphael was torn. It seemed like a harmless thing, just a small favor for Linda. And she was also right. There was plenty of opportunity in the business and Timothy could be scoring any number of valuable books on the internet, selling them and not even telling Raphael. He probably did already. So then this would be all right. He could make Linda happy and not get taken advantage of by Timothy. Yes. That sounds good…but his mind wasn't satisfied with that. Something didn't feel right. On the other side, he had shaken hands with Timothy. They had a deal. He didn't want to cheat or betray Timothy: it just wasn't right.

Raphael looked at Linda, sitting next to him. The cell phone rang. In that same moment as the ringer sounded, Raphael knew what to do and proceeded to include Timothy in the new find from the La Marche cave at Lussac-les-Chateaux. Linda, of course didn't like that, accusing him of betrayal.

Second Story: Inheritance

Terrence stood next to the teller window waiting for the bank clerk to return. She had gone off to verify the signature on the account and when she returned Terrence could tell immediately that the signature had checked out, as he knew it would.

"OK, Mr. Mastine, everything seems to be in order. Your great uncle's inheritance was transferred into your account yesterday and the funds are available now. What would you like me to do? The teller was polite and professional and also eager to complete the transaction and see the next person in line. Terrence, on the other hand, was still thinking about how this impossible largesse had just appeared, out of the blue, like a miracle. He continued to stare.

"Mr. Mastine," asked the teller again, "is there anything else I can do for you?" This time the question was a little more direct, a little more impatient. It snapped him out of his small reverie. "Thank you, that'll be all." he answered and turned around to leave.

He did not know his uncle very well. His parents had always refereed to his father's younger brother as Alvie, though his real name was Salvatore. He was the black sheep of the family, leaving home at 18 to become an artist, traveling the world pursuing fame and fortune. His father would get a Christmas card, usually sometime in January, from some godforsaken place in the middle of nowhere. Never a letter or even a note inside the card. His grandmother pined for Alfie until the day she died. Granny Cara, as she was called, would sit and tell stories of all the amazing and magical places her Alvie had been. Of course she was making this up as no one knew what had become of him except that he always sent Christmas cards in January.

Terrence was the only surviving family member, at least that anyone knew about. There was Rudolfo, of course, his father's illegitimate child. The attorneys and custodians of his uncle's estate did not know of Rudolfo's existence or he would surely have been included in the trust his uncle had set up.

As it turned out, his long lost uncle Salvatore had become quite a wealthy man, having made a name for himself in Europe where he accumulated art and property in a dozen different countries that, when finally liquidated by the trust custodians, added up to almost a million dollars. While he always knew of the existence of his father's illegitimate child, there was an unwritten agreement not to talk about it.

After his mother died, Terrence reached out to Rudolfo and they began to spend time with each other. Rudolfo had become an accountant in a small company and had a large family that he struggled to raise on an accountant's salary. Terrence had retired from the US Marine Corp and lived off his pension. But now…this huge fortune had come to him.

It began to occur to Terrence that it was unfair that he receive the entire inheritance and that Rudolfo, the only other living heir to Uncle Salvatore's fortune, not get anything. But Terrence also felt very strongly that he didn't want to share it, wanted to keep it all for himself and his wife.

In this way the months flew past. Unable to resolve these obviously conflicted feelings, Terrence started avoiding contact with Rudolfo and finally did not accept the invitation for him and his wife to go to Christmas dinner at their house. Slowly their relationship faded and after a year and a half they ceased having any contact at all.

Chapter 2 The Sunset District

Ricardo was born into a middle class Italian family in New York, just after the Second World War. His parents, originally from the fishing village **Positano,** near Naples on the Italian coast, settled in the Sheepshead Bay neighborhood of Brooklyn, where they grew a business specializing in private and commercial boat charters for deep sea fishing excursions.

Susan was born a few years later in Woodmere, a rich suburb just north of New York. Her father was a real estate broker and had divorced Susan's mother two years earlier, when he ran off with a young woman the same age as his daughter.

Susan and Ricardo fell in love and got married. They adopted a dog, a cat, a car, furniture and friends, and led a perfectly normal contemporary life. But slowly, as they matured, their interests, and their lives, began to move in different directions. They liked different music, different food, different TV programs. They liked to do different things on their days off.

Susan started taking art classes at the local community college where she met Travis. One day Travis came back with Susan after class and they stayed in the kitchen drinking coffee and talking and laughing. Ricardo stayed in the living room reading and watching TV, feeling awkward and estranged.

One night, Susan didn't come back from class. As the late-night minutes went by, powerful new feelings began to rise up from Ricardo's gut. First there was anger, then there was more anger, then his mind began visualizing Susan and Travis together. Unrecognizable, powerful and painful surges began to erupt from his solar plexus as anger turned deeper and darker. Pacing the room, he started throwing objects at the brick fireplace, smashing glasses and cups. Susan came back the next day and started fighting. He was losing his grip on reality and, after three days of relentless arguing and fighting, Ricardo left and moved into a hotel.

Very soon after, Travis moved into his house and, as Ricardo kept imagining it, onto the bed which he and Susan had bought with their wedding money. The recurring image of Travis fucking his wife on his own bed was overwhelming and more than his fractured and jealous heart could handle. Day and night, he saw them together, laughing, eating, fucking, laughing, eating, fucking, laughing, eating, fucking. His obsessive mind was out of control.

"Get over it," his friends would say, to deaf ears.

Then, one day, Susan left a recorded message telling him that she was pregnant. Hearing this from her, like that, in that way, on that particular day, pushed Ricardo over some psychological cliff and into a very dark and hateful abyss. This intense feeling was categorically different than the humiliation, pain, ongoing anger, and maniacal jealousy that was his daily mental state: it was hate- not merely anger or rage but hate- why people kill each other. He hated Susan and Travis with such an all-blinding and all-consuming dark malevolent hatred that it overwhelmed him, consumed him. The pain and humiliation was so enormous, so completely overwhelming, that it put Ricardo over the edge of his own humanity.

He had only one thought: his mind was numb, seething in anger, his teeth chattering, his stomach completely battered and tied in knots, with hatred and revenge frothing from his lips. He had to stop this ongoing assault. He couldn't take it anymore.

He arrived at his old house on Water Rock Ave. in the late afternoon and parked across the street, waiting for Susan to come home, ready to confront her and Travis. As he sat there in a daze, his mind kept going over the situation endlessly, in a loop: the first time she went to the ceramics class, the first time she brought him home, the first time they spent the day together, the first time she stayed out late, the last time he saw her, the phone call telling him she was pregnant, the image of them fucking on his bed. Then the images would repeat themselves.

As waves of anguish swept over his entire body, and as his blood boiled with hatred and revenge, his out-of-control mind was lost in a hellish whirlpool of negative energy. Slowly the outside sky got dark, but darker still was the hatred and rage that enveloped him. "Where are they?" he screamed to himself, "Where the fuck are they?"

He hated her and he hated Travis…he wanted to hurt them, kill them, make them finally stop hurting him. In this way the hours passed as Ricardo squirmed in a slimy pool of grime in one of the rooms of his personal hell.

After several hours of self-tortured agony, and suddenly aware of what he was about to do- get into a fight with Susan and Travis- he became overwhelmed with huge convulsions of shame and remorse. He wanted to hurt her, the one person in the world he truly loved. His entire body began convulsing again, and he had to breathe deeply just to stop his brain from exploding.

He had to get out of there. Numb and exhausted, desperate for safety and sleep, he turned the car on and mindlessly began the long drive home. He felt like someone had taken a leaden sledgehammer and pounded at every part of his body- his solar plexus, his navel, his head. He hurt everywhere.

When Ricardo got home, he started to vomit from the sickness of his own self-hatred and self-loathing. He vomited until even the bile was gone, until his insides were bloody and raw. It felt to him like he was expelling his entire knotted existence, his entire compulsion to possess, the entire karmic distortion that kept bringing him the same infidelity, the same betrayal, the same dishonesty, the same emptiness, year after year, lifetime after lifetime.

It was never the same for Ricardo after that. Life went on, but coming face to face with his demon, right there in hell's demon pit, more afraid and loathsome than he ever imagined possible, was a transformative experience.

The ongoing internal resonance of having experienced his broken body, and owning the pathetic and distorted network of raw emotion that lay deep inside his soul, broke apart the foundation of who he thought he was and awakening in him the realization of the fundamental ambiguity of what it meant to be alive. He was compelled to own this dark side, make friends with his demon, merge with the universal pain and suffering of all human beings.

In the end, many years later, he came to understand the great gift Susan and Travis had given him. True friends and soulmates.

Chapter 3 Charity

Thomkins is standing over Rawlins' shoulder watching him transcribe numbers from one ledger to another. Rawlins was meticulous in penmanship and accuracy of transcription and it irritated him that Thomkins was standing so close.

"Mr Thomkins, sir, is there anything I can do for you?" Rawlins said as politely as he could, trying very hard to not give away his distaste of the man. Rawlins continued to transcribe the numbers, making sure it was seamless.

"Just checking up on your ledgers, Rawlins. There's been some irregularities in the bank accounts recently and I'm trying to get to the bottom of it."

"Sir, you can't think that anything I have done is irregular." Rawlins responded with a calculated amount of indignation. "You have certainly checked my transcriptions with your double entry proof system, Tell me what irregularities you have found and perhaps I can help." Thomkins hadn't found anything in reviewing Rawlins' account to justify his suspicion that Rawlins was behind the irregularities. He just couldn't think of anyone as smart as Rawlins or who could be in a position to execute the theft and hide it from the auditors.

He had to find another way to discover how Rawlins was skimming the money. On a hunch he decided to examine Rawlins' personal life to see if the missing money showed up there. Thomkins hired the Private Investigating firm, Somerset & Somerset to follow and trace Rawlins, hoping to uncover the illegal activity. Over the next several months, John Somerset discovered Rawlins' second life: he was a member of a small church and helped administer an orphanage for abandoned children. When Somerset inquired further he discovered that Rawlins bought all the food, paid all the bills and owned the property where the orphanage was situated. It became obvious very quickly that all the money Rawlins earned, and more, went into the orphanage costs.

One day, when Rawlins was at work, Somerset walked into the orphanage and was met by a group of children in the main room singing Bible verse. Somerset was very moved by the children singing and when he went home he was tormented by the decision he had to make. His job was to find the truth and report it. He knew that but he also knew that if he did that the 23 children in the orphanage would be left without their benefactor and probably wind up on the street, or worse. He had spent 17 years developing his reputation and career and now he was thinking to put that at risk for, for what? To protect someone who was stealing from his client? But those children who would be put onto the street, what law protected them? The sad fact was there was none.

He visited other orphanages to see if the children could be moved there but they were all over capacity due to the flu that had swept the country two years earlier. One night, on his way home, Somerset was accosted on the street by two young children who appeared sick and starving. He grabbed them, hailed a carriage, and, despite their ongoing protest, brought them to Rawlins' orphanage. Rawlins opened the door and after a brief conversation, Rawlins agreed to take the children, knowing there really wasn't any room.

"They'll have to sleep on the floor but we will look after them," Rawlins said after a few moments. They won't go hungry." Somerset was taken aback by Rawlins' generosity and made a donation to the orphanage on his way out.

Somerset reported back to Thomkins that Rawlins was innocent of any wrongdoing and that he lived the simple life of an accountant who was active in his local church. Around that same time, donations for the orphanage began increasing and Rawlins began taking less and less from Thomkins' company. At one point that activity ceased completely. Rawlins left the company in the next year in order to run the orphanage full time.

Slowly, Rawlins and Somerset became friends and twenty years later they were administering half a dozen orphanage facilities. Somerset had a knack for getting donors and developed a large philanthropic base for the orphanages. Thomkins came to believe it was the bank itself that was stealing and, though he tried and tried to have them investigated, no one wanted to know about it.

Several years again later, through a completely separate series of events, Thomkins himself became a donor to the orphanage. Was he surprised to see Rawlins and Somerset so fully involved. Surprisingly, he was not at all suspicious of any wrongdoing and thought it was merely by chance that the three of them had met up.

The orphanages created and sustained by Rawlins and others became part of a huge social movement that swept through England in the mid1800s. Rawlins's name was forgotten as the church and government agencies began to take care of this problem. Rawlins, Somerset, and Thomkins died peacefully in their old age surrounded by their loved ones.

Chapter 4: The Time of Samoya

Rogelio was walking down Broadway in New York on a spring morning after a night of rain and thunderstorm. The streets were still wet; the thunderstorm had cleaned the grime from the surface and there was a freshness in the air. He had walked these streets many times, from the subway to the office building and from the office complex back to the subway. He rarely looked at anyone and no one looked at him. People kept to themselves.

Rogelio was guilty of this coldness and distance as well. He lived with his wife, Teodora, in an old public warehouse that had been reclaimed and converted into condominiums. He and Teodora had been married for 6 years and their love for each other was deep and connected. While they both had a spiritual striving, Teodora kept these aspirations inside, choosing to be with God in quiet and solitude. Rogelio, on the other hand, had a very externalized spirituality. He was involved in various "new age" groups and joined online chat rooms that discussed these subjects.

In the middle of these few blocks, in the middle of New York City, no one had time or inclination to meet or connect with anyone they might happen to be passing along in the street. So it came as a huge surprise to Rogelio the day he met Samoya while crossing the intersection at 49th street and Fifth Avenue. He was going west; she was going east. The light had just changed to green and a swarm of people began crossing the intersection. When he passed her initially he didn't notice, but several steps later he felt a huge tug at his attention, and he looked back over his shoulder. He didn't know what he was looking for, or at. Samoya had the identical experience (although she would say much later that she knew.) She turned her head over her shoulder and looked back as well. Not more than 3 seconds passed. Their eyes met but immediately the crush of traffic forced them to continue walking. And that was that.

Two years later, just before the spring equinox, Rogelio was attending a Music Festival in Central Park. Running down the sides of the midway fairgrounds were display tables selling everything from cosmetics made from asteroids to elaborate water filtration systems. Other booths included sacred objects from Tibet, prayer scarves from India and various gongs, bells, and digereedoos. At the far end of the meadow were covered tables with an assortment of strangely dressed individuals doing tarot readings, psychic readings, numerology readings, hand readings and astrology readings.

Rogelio slowly made his way down to that end of the meadow. While he didn't go to the festival to get a reading per se, he was always interested to see the readers. From time to time he might exchange readings with one of the vendors, though this was rare because mostly they were very busy with clients.

Strolling past the reader tables, he walked past one table draped in purple cloth with an easel behind it displaying a sign that said Mystic Visions: Readings and Healings. He had not seen this particular reader at previous shows and stood there for a minute observing. The reader was a woman, middle age, with a black shawl around her shoulders. He couldn't see her face, as she was turned slightly to the side, filling out some papers in her notebook. Someone came up to her table and she turned around to face him, and after a brief conversation she beckoned the man to be seated. When the man sat down Rogelio was able to see the woman's face directly.

His eyes had to blink several times before he could believe what he saw. It was the same woman he had passed on the street in midtown two years earlier. He smiled broadly to himself, but moved off to the side as she began the reading with her client. Slightly euphoric, he walked around the meadow in a daze for the 20 minutes it took for the client to get his reading and leave. When she stood up as the client left, Rogelio could see her full body. Her black hair hung down onto her shoulders and her eyes were slightly slanted, almost oriental, but she was definitely European. She looked healthy and vibrant, was curvy and slim but not skinny, and had an infectious smile.

She said hello to the people walking past, waiting for her next customer. When he came closer to the table, she turned her attention to him, smiling broadly.

"Hello." he said meekly, not wanting to seem too eager.

"Hi." she said back quickly with a warm tone in her voice. "Do you want a reading?" He thought for a moment only. "Yes, that would be great. How much?"

"It's twenty dollars for each 15 minutes." she replied.

"Great, that would be great," he said.

"Please sit down," she said as she motioned him into the chair across her table. "Have you ever had a Tarot reading before?"

"Yes, I've been involved with the metaphysical community for some time. I've been to these shows before but this is the first time I've seen you here," he mumbled.

She was holding the Tarot deck, randomly shuffling the cards as she spoke. "Yes, this is the first time I've been to one of these Fairs. Mostly I have been reading privately for clients." She completed the shuffling and placed the deck face down in the middle of the table, then stared at him, a fierce and penetrating look that made him feel almost naked, emotionally naked.

"Do you have any particular question in mind," she asked matter-of-factly. "Something you want to know? I don't predict the future, so don't ask me those kind of questions."

"Can you read the past?" he asked, suddenly feeling adventurous.

"Yes, I know the past and can see into the akashic record. Is that what you want?" she asked him with keen interest. "A past life reading?"

She continued. "You want to know if the visions you have of Egyptian temples are true accounts of past-life recall or a made up story?" she asked him. That is where he knew her from.

"But, how did you know that, how did you know that was my question?" he mumbled incoherently, amazed at her intuition.

"I knew it as soon as I saw you. We were crossing the street and my entire consciousness was thrown back in time to when we were crossing the inner courtyard of the temple in Luxor. And now here we are, talking to the oracles again. Just like we did then!"

She shuffled the tarot deck, laid out 12 cards in the classic Celtic Cross spread, and began. He tried to listen but all he could do was watch her mouth move, watch her hands move the cards around the table, watch her eyes dart back and forth between the cards. And then, suddenly, the reading was over. He did not remember a single word from the reading and had no clue what she had said. All he could see was her beautiful face, elegant fingers, and dark piercing eyes.

When she gathered up her deck and put her hands on the table, he ot up and stood there. He reached into his pocket and put a twenty-dollar bill on the table which she took and put into the fanny pack around her waist. "Thank you" they both uttered at the same time. All he could do was stand there, like an idiot, his heart racing and beating loudly, staring at her ruby red lips and the crystal pendant that hung down onto the top of her breasts. She smiled at him.

Over the next two years, their friendship grew closer, even while their daily lives stayed far apart. He was happily married to Teodora and loved her deeply. Samoya was single and had many lovers. They would meet at the Fairs or various Workshops around town, but they never touched, never embraced in the lover's dance. Slowly their friendship and emotional intimacy deepened.

They were a perfect match, sharing similar interests in metaphysics besides for that common history in the Egyptian Temples. They spoke the same language, came from the same little corner of the knowing universe, sharing a common vision of the godhead. At first, Rogelio shared these new experiences, this new friendship, with Teodora who was very generous, and supported Rogelio in this friendship. Contrary to societal norms about friendship between married men and single women, she trusted Rogelio and despite subtle waves of jealousy and possessiveness, she acknowledged Rogelio his freedom. She knew that to prevent or inhibit his friendship with Samoya would only drive them closer and into secrecy. Still it was hard seeing her husband, her lover, her best friend, spend time with another woman. Rogelio told her repeatedly that they were only friends and were working on writing a book on metaphysics. This was a plausible reason for them getting together and Teodora believed him, believed in his faithfulness.

And he was faithful, even as his time with Samoya increased over the next months, as the book project, and then, a series of workshops based on the book, began to take shape. They talked on the phone constantly and he sometimes went to visit her at her apartment, just outside the City. Though he never stayed over, they would sometimes work late, sometimes go to dinner, sometimes drink too much wine. They were also aware of how they appeared in public, so friendly, intimate in their laughter and closeness. But they were both aware of the impossibility of the situation and not much was said about it.

One day they were practicing specific exercises they wanted to teach in their next Workshop titled Human Energy Systems. This particular exercise involved two people lying on their backs with their feet up and the bottoms of the feet pressing against the bottoms of the feet of the person across from them. Samoya wanted to show it to Rogelio so he could see the various ways this exercise could morph into more complex exercises that she had in mind. Lying on their backs, on the floor in Samoya's living room, they put the soles of their feet together and began to push against the other's pressure. Sole to sole they began making small circles in the air with their feet while maintaining a constant pressure against the other person's foot. Rogelio didn't know if it was the wine or the body motion, if it was the incense or the perfume, if it was his desire rising or her desire rising, but the motion in their legs and the dance of desire between their energy fields suddenly transformed the simple leg exercise into a deep physical and sexual experience.

Like powerful magnets brought close, their bodies began to draw closer. He reached over and with his arm around her shoulder, brought her face close to his. Her lips, so beautiful with ruby red lipstick, waited in suspense. Her hands had come around the back side of his neck and brought him closer to her. Passion raged in their blood. Desire raged in their bodies.

At that moment, the same ancient memory crossed their merged minds. They had the same awareness, a recall of the same ancient sin that had plagued thousands of years of their human experience. They saw the temple gardens, the farmer's hut in rural China, the fishing village in a Neanderthal dreamscape. They saw the choices made and remade:

the victory of betrayal over love, of desire over loyalty and truth. As they looked at each other with eternal eyes, they embraced even more tightly, the molecules of their soul bodies merging in a blistering heat of passion and connectedness. They held on in this way for several long moments, relishing the divine union of souls that they were experiencing. Then, after several moments, their energy bodies began to slowly separate. Slowly they pulled apart.

Rogelio put his shoes on, gathered his books and walked to the door. Silently they embraced one more time. Both knew that they wouldn't see each other anymore, that they had crossed an impossible boundary. It didn't need to be said. They held their embrace a long time, holding each other with deep passion and feeling. Silently she opened the door where he left quietly. Their work was complete.

When he got home, back to the warehouse in the City, Teodora was fast asleep. He woke her up and they talked and made love. Soon after, circumstances forced Samoya to move and she left no forwarding address. Rogelio never saw her again in that lifetime.

Chapter 5 The Visitor

Our little hermitage is tucked away in the mountain and is hard to find even if you are looking for it. So it came as a mild surprise that, one day just after the snow had melted, a stranger appeared at the front gate. We all noticed that there was something different about him: the way he carried himself, and his mannerisms were simple and precise, with no wasted effort. There was a lightness to him, as though on a hot and uncomfortable day a cool scented wind had come across the nostrils. He called himself 'the traveler,' and he asked if he could stay with us.

After two days, a rhythm emerged. Each morning, when the sun rose over the eastern mountain he would sit near the old well in the upstairs courtyard and, after a few minutes, begin chanting. His chant echoed throughout the small hermitage, and soon all the monks and nuns came and sat and chanted with him. He recited the regular chants, scriptures we recite every day: sacred prayers for protection, for well-being, for world peace, for liberation. But this was different. His voice was so clear, vibrating with such compassion and knowledge that the deeper meaning of the words somehow penetrated our minds more profoundly.

On the fourth day, after a particularly intense and powerful chanting, one of the nuns asked the traveler if he would speak about the nature of existence. He glanced over at the old abbot who nodded his head and smiled. The traveler closed his eyes and began speaking.

"When we are born we immediately grasp for the objects of the world and throughout our lives we continue grasping. Even before we are born we are grasping for the objects of the world and then come into these bodies in order to succeed in our desire to grasp at these wondrous objects. We're good at this and our grasping has no bounds. At first we grasp for small things- a little milk, some touching. Then we grasp for larger things- toys, clothing, family, certain kinds of feelings, all manner of possessions. And since we are so good at this, trained over and over, we usually succeed in getting the objects we are grasping for." It was so quiet, even the light wasn't moving.

"But when we succeed in getting the object of our grasping, we are satisfied for only a little while and then we grasp again at another object. This, then, is the basic nature of our existence: we are preprogrammed to grasp at objects, then become disappointed in not being able to hold on to those objects, and then grasp at the next object. One thing after another, driving the unrelenting urgency to grasp and possess. That's part of the system software that runs the hardware of our physical existence, and into which is embedded specific code for dissatisfaction and existential discontent."

"On their own level, even the celestial beings are dissatisfied: grasping, wanting, even if it is only desiring salvation, they are incomplete in their own essence, wanting more, more experience, more compassion, more salvation. Even the monks are grasping- for food, for wisdom, for liberation." Then he said more slowly- "The whole Creation is grasping, reaching, desiring, its own manifestation and fulfillment." The traveler let those last words linger. "There is no shame in this. It's how the universe is constructed. God made it this way." he concluded before a long silence.

Then he continued: "And what happens when we do get the objects we are grasping for? The child gets the cookie, then wants another one. The person with the fancy clothes will grow tired of them and then want new clothes. Or he'll want the next computer or video game. The businessman gets the fancy house but soon he wants the adjacent orchard. He gets the orchard but soon wants an airplane to see everything he owns. We will never be satisfied. Even when we get the objects of our grasping, we will finally become dissatisfied in our experience, and then continue to seek out other objects to grasp."

"We continue to grasp at life, at the objects of life, even into our deathbed. And then, with ongoing desire we find our way into a new body, perfectly re-adapted to fulfill our desire for grasping. And we grasp and we grasp. And we crave and we crave. If we look closely and are honest with ourselves, we see that in our lives, and in all sentient lives, on whatever planet or plane of existence, barely a moment goes by which is not governed by this operational imperative. So our condition is clear and simple. We are pre-programmed grasping machines, forever destined to be dissatisfied with the circumstances of our lives, destined to grasp again and again in a never ending cycle of desire, dissatisfaction and then renewed desire."

At that point the traveler closed his eyes and smiled. How many times had we heard this discourse on the roots of suffering? But it was never so personal, so real. It was never about my suffering, about my ongoing discontentment, never about me, always about others and somehow, as monks and nuns, we were detached from that, beyond that, maybe even a little superior. But this traveler's words pierced right into our hearts, into my heart, and I understood this fundamental truth in a way I had never understood it before.

He said we needed to develop an "ecology of mind" for cleaning up the toxic mess of unresolved desire that we inherited, while at the same time nurturing a healthy spiritual growth by aligning our center of being with the higher supramental frequency, just now becoming available on the various physical planes of existence.

"Pull the plug on the obsolete program," he said, "and dislodge the virus of discontent. Transform the nature of your existence. New possibilities exist that never existed before."

"But first we have to become aware of these subconscious subroutines that bind us to this sense of permanency. We have to throw the light of our awareness onto this ancient biological machinery, see the switches and mechanisms that were necessary for survival, at some point perhaps, but are no longer needed. We have to bring our entire body/mind singularity up to this new heightened level of conscious awareness."

"Something has changed in the universe," he kept repeating. "There is a new immanence, a new possibility. We can consciously choose it, make specific, willful intention to bring this Awakened Intelligence into our everyday reality."

Then the visitor became quiet, closed his eyes and began a slow chant in a language none of us had ever heard. It was something mysterious and sacred and beautiful all at once. It was as though the sounds themselves were solid objects, pieced together like a mosaic, a three-dimensional song that extruded light and color, scent and sound.

After an hour of chanting, as though no time had passed, he continued where he left off. "When the core principle and operating software that has informed sentient existence for the last ten thousand years is shifted, a new evolution becomes possible. Not just possible, but inevitable."

The traveler became quiet as his vision of a future world governed by these spiritual principles lit up our minds. From the existing mountaintop, with its evolving sentient consciousness, he showed us the next mountaintop, across the wide valley of time and destiny, where the accelerating sentient evolution would reach another milestone on its timeless journey to unite with the original divine consciousness.

The traveler stayed with us a few more days, mostly in quiet contemplation. Then, one morning the traveler left. Life continued on in our little hermitage. But everything was different; the very molecules in the air were different, even the smell of sweat was different. Everything had an aura of aliveness, of presence.

Chapter 6 Stephanie

When Stephanie decided to get born again she first contacted Alishah, her spirit guide and mentor. She wanted to create a significant life, bringing together the diverse life threads that she had been cultivating through her multiple lifetimes. With Alishia's help, she began reviewing her previous 8000 years of sentient experience. She revisited the whole range of lifetimes: lifetimes when she had been generous, kind and creative as well as other lifetimes when she had been selfish, cruel and myopic. She'd been part of more wars, conflicts and genocides than she wanted to remember. But she did remember. Alishah made her remember and made sure she saw the full picture of her actions- good and bad. She saw, for example, how she would be born in one tribe, commit atrocities against a second tribe and then immediately get born into the second tribe as the victim of her "former" self. Or, once when she was a merchant she saw how she stole the objects created by an artisan. Immediately, upon that artisan's death, she was born as a daughter of that same artisan who, because of that theft, had been forced into a life of servitude and poverty.

Alishah showed her everything; nothing was left hidden. Some lifetimes were wretched, some filled with grace and wonder. She saw that her prime directive, what her soul wanted most, over those thousands of years, was to manifest Beauty as an expression of her spirit body. She saw the wall paintings in the caves and the flower gardens she had tended as a landscaper in ancient China.

As visions of her loved ones passed before her celestial eye, she saw how she would arrange life after life with her soul mates, Raja and Tendo. She saw, also, the betrayals and convoluted layers of feelings and actions and reactions that the three of them had created, the karma that kept bringing them back into suffering.

While she reviewed these stories with the help of Alisha, she tried to find meaning in these experiences. But meaning was elusive. How had she become so compelled to the sentient experience with its inevitable tragedy and death? Sometimes she died alone; sometimes in misery. Sometimes she died in the lap of her loved ones, after a long and fruitful life. Sometimes death was instantaneous; sometimes drawn out over years and years. She saw how she always resisted death, how she clung to life so tenaciously, and how, after finally dying, always wanted to get reborn, to have more of the experience in her body, whatever the cost or consequence.

Only moments passed. It was really too much to apprehend. The overwhelming amount of simultaneous conflicting emotions ravaged her entire spirit body. She cried from a deep powerful pain and laughed with an unequivocal joy in the same moment. It was only Alisha's standing there, holding her core, that enabled Stephanie to be present with this multi-dimensional trans-warp experience.

After reviewing this historical record, she saw the overall pattern of her experience- from the beginning lives with a dull sentience to an increasingly aware consciousness. But she also saw that she wasn't quite finished, that there were loose ends, unresolved entanglements still dotting the karmic trail.

Suddenly, a huge urgency demanded that she take a leap and jump to the next level of her soul's power. All she knew was that that was the only thing she wanted as her entire spirit became laser focused. There was nothing whimsical about this huge decision- to bring all the residual karmic forces together in one lifetime. But the laws of karma are complicated, unsentimental, devastatingly impersonal and mathematical. Nonetheless, Stephanie was determined: a big push to a final and full resolution of her karmic entanglements. She felt Alisha strongly in the background, helping her design her next life.

Slowly a plan took shape and she began to form a rough outline- the people she would meet, the time and locations of significant events. And then there was the astrology that needed to be assembled to help accomplish these enormous goals. She had to distill from these hundreds and hundreds of lives and thousands and thousands of embedded karmic capsules the main purpose and direction that her ten thousand year journey had been leading her.

Alisha moved into the background as the full force and power of Stephanie's soul body began to compose her next life. She waited for the planets to align, waited for the DNA strands to synch, waited for the womb to be ready…

Book 7
Pacific

Chapter 1 Mission Bay

The trees appear relatively small when silhouetted against the massive reinforced concrete and steel bio-tech buildings dotting the Mission Bay campus. Mission Bay was a sparkling new university built on former marshland at the edge of the Pacific Ocean on San Francisco Bay. Each building, housing its own bio-tech discipline was creatively different in design, color, size of window and exterior trim. All the buildings morphed together as a training ground for the next generations of biotech scientists and engineers.

It was here that Aung incarnated in a physical body through an entire birth/death cycle and not merely as a walk-in. When he jumped into his mother's womb he immediately began replicating and differentiating the DNA strands necessary to fulfill the lofty purpose of this incarnation-to present to the world an articulate mathematical vision demonstrating the measurable interconnectedness between all biologically based organisms. Similar to E=mc2 that connected Matter, Energy and Light, this formula would connect Mind, Biology and Consciousness.

His mother and father were not aware of any of this and Ankara grew up mostly normal in a mostly normal condominium complex in Trenton, New Jersey. He seemed to have a natural aptitude for various subjects, especially science and mathematics, and so progressed through the school systems, into post graduate work, teaching, and then tenure at the newly constructed, reinforced steel and concrete biotech nucleus still known a hundred years after its original construction as Mission Bay. His specialty was the mathematics underlying biogenesis, known more formally as the Bio Origination Theory (BOT).

The published works on this subject all pointed to the need for the original Big-Bang- in which all matter in the known universe exploded out from a single point- to have had an a-priori code for biologic life embedded in that singularity. According to Ankara's theory, specific bio-incipient Planck particulates transformed over the next 15 billion years into biologic life as we know it, demonstrating that it was not merely an accident of nature. The Bio Origination Theory specifically indicated that these micro points of biomass were present in the Big Bang. The question that had baffled generations- "Where did life come from?" could now be answered. BOT theory, in demonstrating that it has always been here, neutralized once and for all the centuries old dichotomy between Evolutionary Science and Creationism as descriptions for the origin of the universe.

Ankara had been brought up in the thick of this question. His parents, especially his father, were avowed creation theory advocates, believing that the Jehova God had created the world, more or less sequenced like the seven days of biblical Genesis. They thought that the Darwinian theories of evolution and their elaborate pseudo-scientific consequences, missed the key reality: that all creation originated with the Genesis theory of divine intervention.

On the other hand, his maternal grandparents believed very strongly in the scientific revelation, even to its atheistic inevitability. He had sat at many dinners where his father and grandfather would go at it, discussing finer and finer detail, co-relating the worlds of biology, geology, neurology, anthropology with other cross-discipline subject areas. With his mathematical bent, he sought out basic fundamental axioms to describe the truths he heard over the kitchen table. He had a small notebook of scribbled mathematical formula that he carried with him everywhere.

This interest finally led Ankara to the Mission Bay School for Cosmological Research and his current area of focus: the evolution of mind. He felt like he was close to a breakthrough, co-relating E, M and c as they approach the Origin Point (O), the preta-moment of the Big Bang. His theory stated that Mind and Life were also present at the Origin point, not only Matter and Light.

Besides for his theoretical research, Ankara also had a full load of teaching. His Origins class was required for all post docs. Not that it needed to be required; it was a favorite on campus. He particularly enjoyed the discussion groups that formed around the class, often meeting in students' dorms or library anterooms. The library itself was housed in the student services building along with the gym, the pools, the cafe and the ping pong tables. One day, as Ankara was getting lunch at the café, he sat down at the table with some of his students, including Rain and Rain's friend, Sienna.

They were in the middle of a conversation about the latest discovery- water on the Vegan moon, Irodios and the apparent proliferation of water throughout the galaxy. The question they were all talking about was: If there is so much water, why were there not more green planets, like Earth,, proliferating?

"Maybe we just can't see them…maybe it's in a slightly shifted dimension, not within the huminoid perceptual field…" Rain was saying.

"So the planet only appears barren… it's just an illusion and it's really green? is that what you're saying?" poked Sienna

"No, other dimensions aren't illusory, they are green on their own vibratory level. They only just vibrate at a slightly shifted frequency compared to the frequency range we experience here, in these bodes. Those aren't the same things. If you…"

"Is this dimension we are in, here and now, sitting at this table, illusory?" playfully interjected Ankara

Thinking for a moment. Rain replied, "No, this is the real thing. Pinch yourself. See if it hurts. That's not illusory pain."

"So how many of these dimensions do you think there are?" asked Ankara

"Well I can count nine manifest dimensions," answered Rain, "but I'm sure there are more, I'm sure there are etheric planes that I can't see but I bet Sienna can see them." And, using her highly tuned mental power she was able to see beyond the nine planes into the incipient worlds, still unformed and tenuous, sitting across the wide cosmic emptiness.

They all sat there quietly for several long moments, absorbed in Sienna's vision of the vastness of the cosmic landscape. But the urgency to enlightenment notwithstanding, reality called them back into their bodies, to their lunch table and that present moment. It was time to get back to class So gathering their books and jackets, they all stood up, acknowledged each other with a smile and went off on their separate ways.

For sentient beings on the billions of worlds across the trillions of galaxies, physical evolution had reached a utilitarian perfection. The physical body, whether on terrestrial planets, water or methane planets, though still prone to old age and death, had matured into the perfect vehicle for manifesting the ongoing cosmic evolution- the evolution of mind. Ankara, his students, and countless others around the earth and throughout the galaxy, were actively embodying a new supramental consciousness, a level of ascended awareness as different from the ordinary sentient mind as the ordinary mind is different from the monkey mind, which itself had evolved out of a more rudimentary consciousness, going back to the dawn of creation.

The cosmic evolution of sentient beings had reached the next step on the long evolutionary ladder. Rain, Sienna, and their friends and teachers were participating in the dawn of a new civilization, a new actualization, emerging quietly out of a ten thousand year slumber.

Chapter 2 Sausalito

The hills rising over the Bay were bathed in a low afternoon sun, reflecting magenta and crimson into the clouds lingering on the western horizon. Saki recalled vividly the image of other hills rising from other oceans that were the shoreline of the ancient continent. She could see other houses sitting on the edges of the cliffs on the imagined coast just as she could see the real houses rising on the Tiburon Hill. She pondered other similarities to those ancient times…particularly the predictions. This Bay Area is earthquake country and the houses are built to withstand different levels of tremors, shocks and aftershocks. The houses on Atlantis, especially the southern side, were also built to withstand the earth movements that had been predicted during the last hundred years of that world. She remembered those last days so vividly: how the frequency of earth tremors had accelerated and become more and more severe, how hysteria had overwhelmed the population as the seriousness of the calamity had become evident. The continent was breaking apart and sinking.

No one really expected the calamitous extent of the devastation, that within 5 days the entire continent would have become submerged, that no matter whether your house was built of straw, iron or crystal it would have been torn apart. No one expected the particularly close passing of the asteroid, later named Harakan, simultaneous with a 23 degree pole shift. It was too much.

But Randy didn't know this was about to happen, living self-reliantly three days into the wilderness with Saki, on the Crystal Island, just off the south shore. He blamed himself for what happened, how their beautiful house on the hill, overlooking the crystal sanctuary, slid into the ocean on the eve of the final upheaval. Everything he loved all crushed in the weight of the stone and rock.

He was on a boat, just a half mile off shore, documenting tidal changes from the receding asteroid, when the earth split apart right below his house. First he heard a huge booming sound and suddenly there was chaos. He heard screaming and saw Saki being thrown outward by the force of the exploding crystal and into the mass of debris collapsing around her. Randy watched in horror as his house and sanctuary, his family, and everything he knew and loved was destroyed in a matter of seconds. He didn't have time to say goodbye to Saki, his beloved Saki, who, even though she had betrayed him and fallen in love with Theros, was still his Saki, whom he had promised to love and protect. As the Crystal Sanctuary came apart, with agony of soul, under the shadow of betrayal, and with deep painful feelings of self-hatred and remorse, feeling somehow responsible for the deaths of his family, he watched in despair as they all perished in front of him.

He never forgave himself for this: he just watched them all die. He should have known; he, above all people, should have known. He knew the ground had become unstable. He should have taken them away to safety, reinforced the crystal onyx baseplate, figured something out. What he couldn't have known was that the entire continent was breaking apart; he couldn't have known that there wasn't anything he could have done to save his family, that no human structure survived the crushing weight of the negative gravity of the receding asteroid. Then, suddenly, in the next moment, he was swept up in a huge tsunami and died quickly. In his last mind moment, as his life force quickly dissipated, the twisted guilt and fear arising in his mind became fixated and implanted itself into his karmic DNA.

Saki tried talking to him about it many times, in many different lifetimes, as they played this out and tried to heal those old wounds- guilt, betrayal, terror and loss. Maybe some of it got open to the light of truth; maybe it won't ever be possible to heal all of it. Maybe we have to just live with our suffering, learn to accept the consequences of our actions- maybe this is what brings us closer to God. That's how it was for Randy. It made him less arrogant, more vulnerable, more sensitive, more empathic.

She went on with this memory dream for quite some time as the rhythmic wave pattern of the Bay's eddies and micro currents lulled her into these visions. Opening her eyes and coming back into her body, she looked up and saw the hills rising over the East Bay, now glowing in a golden sunset across the Racooon Straits, Angel Island and San Quentin. Across the water, the waves began kicking up as more of the sun had moved behind the fog bank. She scanned across the Bay Bridge, Treasure Island and the beautiful San Francisco skyline. How she loved this spot, this little corner of the universe; she loved it despite those painful memories of another time and another place.

The weather started getting chillier. Scientists think that the Bay Area will get rocked by another giant earthquake. Probably. She had already been in several smaller earthquakes. But today, this last Friday in May, children are playing and laughing on the grass and people are walking their dogs along the edge of the waterfront. The ferry has returned to pick up the last batch of tourists it had dropped off earlier. The birds are chirping, the water is calm, the hills rising from the Bay are green and houses dot the beautiful landscape. There won't be an earthquake today.

Just then Richard got off the commuter ferry. Today was the day, she had decided, that she would make an initial contact with him. He would typically walk off the ferry, past the stores on Bridgeway and stop at the Starbucks on Prince St for an afternoon latte. But it was what he was reading that had initially attracted her attention: he was reading *Savitri,* an epic poem by the Indian poet-philosopher Sri Aurobindo. He would sit there, sip on his coffee, read some, and then stare out through the glass window, past the street and into the distance beyond the edge of the water.

She had read some of Aurobindo herself. *Savitri*, an epic poem, is the story of two souls, Savitri and Satyavan, who travel through plane after plane of cosmic existence to find and consummate their love. She went over to his table. "Hi," she said in a cracked voice. He looked up and focused his attention.

"Hi," he answered with a smile.

"I see you're reading *Savitri*- wow! such a great story- I love Aurobindo, I never meet anyone who's read this …." Saki said quickly.

"You've read this?" Richard quickly asked, astounded. "I've never met anyone who's read this either!"

They both laughed. "I've only read some of it. I mean it is a thousand pages, but I really like the stanza where Satyavan confronts the Angel of Death and compels him to release his beloved Savitri. Makes me very emotional just thinking about it." she blurted out. '*With deathless eyes he looked upon the eyes of death,*' I just love that line. Very empowering."

Richard was smiling. They went on and on talking about the poem, about Aurobindo, about the great vision this Indian mystic had for the future of mankind. They talked of other teachers, other paths. Over the next several days, as they met again and again at Starbucks, they got to know each more and more. It didn't take very much, after all, considering how well they already knew each other. They slept together a few days later, after a dinner at Martha's in Mill Valley. "Maybe we had a little too much wine, maybe we had a little too much history, but we felt like we were personally living the saga of Savitri and Satyavan," she later wrote in her blog.

"Richard," she mentioned to him several days later at Starbucks, "I want you to meet the rest of my family." He didn't seem surprised. "I told you I live in a house in Bolinas, but I didn't tell you that I live in a—in a …commune."

His body shrunk back ever so slightly. The word 'commune' had become almost a dirty word in the culture, suggesting end-of-the-world cults and fundamentalist-crazy survivalists. Saki went on to describe how her extended family lived together in these several houses near the beach, pooled their finances, ate common meals, shared vehicles, and even clothing, though "we do not share our beds or even our beliefs." She went on, "what we do share is our humanity and our striving."

She explained all of this to him as concisely as possible. At one point his arched back eased up, his face relaxed and he listened attentively. She told him about Sash'wa, the founder of the 'Group'. She told him how they had become a legal church in California with a non-profit charter whose "religious" purpose was to do healing and teaching. She told him about the background of the individuals who were part of the group and how they were ordained as ministers in the church, receiving new names like Moonglow and Starhawk, Isis, and Serena of the Light. "Each person is trying in their own way to help bring a higher energy to the planet," she told him. "We travel around the Bay Area and set up 'Healing Days' in various communities, give readings and healings to whoever asks."

Slowly, as Richard began attending healings and group dinners, rituals and parties, he became more intimate with this little family and more fully committed to the path of personal and planetary transformation. Several months later Richard was ordained into the Order of Melchezidek in a freezing cold ritual at Upper Meadow near the top of Mt Shasta and was given the name River. He moved into Transcendence House, a pyramid shaped structure that tilted precariously on a bluff overlooking the Pacific. Saki and River continued to be lovers but lived separately. Life was good.

The following spring a young woman, Beatrice, began hanging out with the group. She had come to several of the Sunday healing rituals and just fit right in with this strange little hippie family. Everyone regarded her as a long lost sister, happily re-surfacing after all these years. Beatrice had been a college athlete until a skiing accident put her on the bench. She had mostly healed herself with a strong yoga practice and was now teaching yoga in Mill Valley. She was also studying "past life regression therapy" at JFK University in Orinda and soon began practicing "regression therapy" on the group. Beatrice and Saki became very close and were always hanging out with River, creating workshops, playing music, cooking group meals. Several months later, when she asked to join the group and become ordained, everyone was very excited. During the naming ceremony, at the time of her initiation into the Order of Melchezidek, Beatrice was ordained as Triad.

Triad became a powerful regression therapist and, several months later, she regressed River. Several past lives came up quickly - Russian, Persian, Chinese. Suddenly, in the middle of their session, River's body began to shake. Sweat formed on his face and he began sobbing, winding up on the floor in a fetal position. "I'm sorry, I'm sorry," he kept mumbling over and over as his sobbing became uncontrollable, his breath erratic and shallow. It went on this way for ten more minutes. Triad kept trying to hold him, but he pushed her away.

The way Triad wrote about it in her book forty years later, after River had died, was that he had begun remembering a particularly powerful end-of-life experience on the Far Mountain, way deep into the akashic memory, at the very beginning of his current ten thousand year journey. She wrote "…and from that regressed edge, he was able to glimpse into an even more remote time, the time before this current round of lives, to a previous ten thousand year cycle. And there, in that last mind moment on the water, at the edge of the Crystal Sanctuary, destruction, guilt, betrayal and helplessness had taken hold of his karmic matrix and penetrated his core, informing life after life and body after body.

She wrote in her book how River had broken down completely then, "crying in deep gasping wails, ten thousand years of pain exploding out in anguish and remorse." This ancient violence, tragedy and guilt, though undeserved, defined the lens and filter through which he had created and experienced his world.

She wrote: "He would always find himself in situations where he felt that he had let his loved ones down and had violated their trust and safety in some way. Time and time again, over thousands of years and lifetimes."

"I began doing forgiveness meditation with him," Triad recounted. "At first it was very superficial, not really penetrating this deeply wounded core. But we worked at it. One day, out of the blue, after a particularly intense session for both of us, I told him that I forgave him."

Triad wrote "Somehow, for some reason, that sparked the memory of a series of lives where he had walked away from his children to go die in foreign wars. All he could see was a picture of this little boy crying in the window, knowing he would never see his father again. Then his mind jumped back to the Sanctuary."

"And River cried 'I abandoned you, betrayed my children, my friends!….life after life…Oh God I just left you! Left you and her to die! Oh my God….I couldn't stop it! The mountain collapsed all around you…I couldn't stop it…'"

Triad wrote "And we held each other and cried for a long time. We worked at this forgiveness, at coming to terms with the fundamental ambiguity in our experience as human beings, resolving deeper and deeper threads in our wounded cores. Slowly, something changed. In the weeks and months that followed it seemed like the center of gravity in River's body had shifted. He stood up straighter and laughed more.

And when he died this time, surrounded by his friends and family, his last words, and presumably the words the angels heard during his transition, was the sacred mantra of forgiveness.

Triad and Saki remained close friends and thought often about River who, really, was never that far away from them.

Chapter 3 Grace

They had been fasting and meditating for the week between Christmas and New Year. It is a holy time, an ending and a beginning, a crack between the worlds. They were sitting in their small living room, quiet, candle lit, reading to each other, discussing the similarities and differences between the different spiritual paths that have been leading humanity up the evolutionary mountain. They were discussing the texture of the trail surfaces - how a south facing trail might be warmer; a north facing trail may be more disciplined, maybe more icy. The mountain's many trails are on all sides, crisscrossing, converging, bifurcating, spiraling. Thousands of trails; new trails laid over older ones, some following the river, others rock strewn and almost impassable. All these paths converging on the same mountain peak: the peak of liberation.

"We have gone down so many miraculous paths," they tell each other. "It feels so close, I can taste it, taste what freedom is like." Now they were near the top of the mountain. After this long journey, after all the years of discipline and practice, they could see the final freedom. Near the top of the mountain, as the trail heads begin to converge, fewer and fewer paths remain. All the thousand trails had merged, converged and morphed into only the few remaining rock strewn paths.

They continue walking. Suddenly, unpredictably, the road narrows and the incline angle of the path gets much steeper. It's hard to maintain traction as their feet begin slipping, the whole weight of gravity pushes them backwards, blocking any forward motion. Then, in the next mind moment, huge rock overhangs suddenly appear out of the mountain on top of them. The paths become all twisted, almost impassable, as they try again….and again to find their way. But the rock overhang keeps stopping them.

"We can never reach the mountaintop," he finally says to her as the hopelessness of the situation becomes more evident, inevitable, non-compromising. "There never has been a way to do this," they realize with an ultimate clarity mixed with great dismay. The mountain paths continue to get steeper, more indistinguishable from the rocky mountain, more impassable. Nature won't allow it.

But "No ! No !" they scream with renewed passion as they thrust back against the unrelenting force of nature. "We have to reach the top, despite the force of cosmic gravity impeding us at this last moment, preventing us from achieving the final freedom. We have to reach the top," they cry to each other.

They are pinned against the underside of the rock overhang and are about to start falling backwards. "We're falling…we'll be crushed by the mountain…" as the rock overhang collapses on top of them: death is at hand. With deathless eyes they meet each other…they have the same thought and with a huge act of will, using leg muscles strengthened by ten thousand years of walking through miles of twisting uphill road, they kick-push themselves off the side of the mountain and leap with abandon into the oxygen and hydrogen.

No time passes.

Suddenly, out of nowhere, a thin rope appears in front of them, just at the edge of their grasp, coming closer. The rope hangs in the sky: it just hangs there… compelling them to grab it. Holding onto the rope, wrapping it around their arms and legs, they stop their fall into oblivion. Suddenly, there they are, suspended in the emptiness, clutching on to a tiny sliver of rope coming out of nowhere, hanging down from the top of the ancient mountain.

In the next moment there is a tug on the rope. They hold on as they are slowly pulled up past the edge of the overhanging rock which had made it impossible to traverse just moments earlier. And then, suddenly, in the next mind moment, they find themselves squatting on top of a flat disc on top of the sacred mountain.

Looking around, they see a large army of what can only be described as light beings throwing ropes over the side of the mountain and, then, after a brief pause, pulling back on the rope, lifting up another human, another sentient, another being, another light body, on to the top of the mountain. Millions and billions of light bodies gathering on the top of the sacred mountain, illuminating the entire Cosmos and transforming Creation.

Chapter 4 The Structured Policy

One of the most unusual lives I experienced around that time was being born into a family in the Northern Mountain Range above the third climactic ring on the cold world of Polonia. It was an ice culture where the air was always in a permafrost. It was one weird place.

I was the third child of Thomas and Madeline. We lived modestly at the end of a long, windy, slightly uphill road, 1-1/2 hours from the town center. The town center itself consisted of a small hardware store, a food warehouse and a meeting room that was used as a combination schoolroom/police station. There was an efficiency to this civic design as only the one building needed to be maintained and heated.

My mother had 6 children- as prescribed in the Structured Policy Manual- 3 boys and 3 girls. We each had our own small room with a bed and table where we spent all our time alone when not otherwise in school or performing the prescribed chores. Once past the initial core learning- reading and arithmetic- the only subject to study before the Science plat- form was the Structured Policy Manual. We had to memorize it entirely, cover to cover. By the time of our maturity date- also prescribed in the Policy Manual based on sex and birth placement, it was fully expected that each of us children would the general sciences and then become ex- pert in one specific field appropriate to our nature- which was also identi- fied in the Manual in the chapter, Science of Neural-stem Programming.

No one questioned this natural progression: learn to read and do arithmetic, memorize the Manual, study the have learned appropriate science, work for the state facility, have a family with six children, work the garden, eat at 7:30 and so on. There just were no deviations from this established sequence and even the thought of deviating never arose.

Our father was very strict in his adherence to the Structured Policy. He would say over and over again "We have done it this way for as many generations as our society has existed and our society has existed for these many generations because we have done it this way." My father came home from his work as a plant engineer at the Food Factory exactly at

4:30 each day, sat with a glass of water and a piece of fruit until 5:00 at which time he would go outside to the small enclosed garden and work the vegetable bins until dusk. My mother, in the meantime, prepared a meal for the entire family to be eaten at 7:30. We would all sit down in our backless chairs while my father recited the appropriate stanza from the Structured Policy Manual before the meal. We ate in silence.

Our mother was also very strict in the application of the Structured Policy. She prepared the pre-assigned Tuesday meal on Tuesday, the Wednesday meal on Wednesday and so on. In the same way, each child had chores that were specifically detailed. On Monday I would clean the fireplace, on Tuesday I would rake the fifty foot hill leading up to the house. On Thursdays my sister would flash iron the table cloths. On Saturdays my two younger brothers would accumulate loose wood from the surrounding forest for the weeks kindling. This was all proscribed very clearly in the Structured Policy Manuals and we were diligent in the performance of these duties.

Life was very simple for our family and our community. We followed the Structured Policy in all phases of life; everything had been thought through and all decisions had been predetermined. All personal relationships proceeded according to the Relationship Book; all conversation proceeded according to the Communication Book and so on. There were never any complaints, disagreements or even discussion about the way of life. Everyone lived this way and this was the way everyone lived. It was very logical, very efficient, very organized. There was never any conflict or disagreement. It worked.

By the time I was 23, I was a fully participating bio-vector in the Structured Policy Power Grid. My sister, Sandia had married the specified third cousin on our mother's side and was now pregnant with her first child- a girl. They had moved into a house exactly similar to the one we grew up in. It was repainted and fresh new curtains and tablecloths were given to them by the community. My sister's husband went off to work at the Tool Factory, came home at 4:30, worked in their garden while she prepared dinner, then they both performed the appropriate chores for that day and then went to bed. Life was simple. Everything got done that needed to get done and nothing was done that wasn't needed.

But for me something was never quite right; I never felt like I belonged in that family or that place. Someone must have made a mistake,

I thought to myself behind closed doors, not even really having a context for what something different might be. But despite this inner (unnamed) alienation, my alignment with the Structured Policy was inviolate and I knew that these were inappropriate thoughts and I continually dismissed them.

My father died accidentally when an earthquake shattered the building where he was working and a huge beam fell on his head. Of course things like this would happen, randomly, from time to time, but this time, I don't know, I began to experience a change in my body that was unusual. My facial muscles changed, my lips sagged at the edges and, unbelievably, my eyes became moist. I couldn't concentrate on the tasks at hand and my mind kept repeating images of my father at the table, my father drinking water, my father doing chores, my father tending a fire or roasting an animal I didn't recognize. What? Roasting an animal in a fire pit? Where did that come from? It's as though my father were there next to me, looming over me, knowing of course that that was not possible. But I just couldn't stop my mind from racing between these thoughts.

But that was also not the whole of it. My husband, while completely focused on his work, his chores, his dutiful attention to our house and his strict application of the Structured Policy, seemed like a total stranger, someone from another country. I barely knew him and when I tried to share this experience of seeing my father, he dismissed it immediately and referred me to a Chapter 6 in the Policy Manual.

I remember speaking to my sisters and brothers about this and all they could say was to reread the Structured Policy Manual, especially Chapter 6, listen to some tapes, and settle into the life that was pre-established for me. Their support must have helped a little bit, but mostly these weird thoughts and feelings continued unabated. Getting no answers at home, or from the people I knew, I secretly searched my father's library (which had been confiscated by the Book Society and now lived in sealed boxes in the basement of the Town HallallHlnhbbhb) for anything that would help me understand my situation and experience and, hopefully, help me to readjust to the correct Structured Program.

Was I ever surprised to find, on my third day of searching through my father's old books, a small volume hidden between some pages in one of the Manuals. It was titled *Feelings and Emotions*. I didn't even know what those words meant. I opened it and began to read.

"For millennia, the superior beings of Polonia have been burdened by a wide range of counterproductive emotions: hatred, anger, sadness, happiness, jealousy, fear, and many more. Because of these conflictve human emotional threads, and their compelling distortion of reality, whole human cultures have been destroyed, and the very existence of those planets have been threatened." What are they talking about, I wondered, as I kept reading.

"Therefore, we have concluded that it is best to program a society where these unnecessary and unhelpful aspects of human behavior have been removed. The Structured Policy, governing every moment of a person's life, leaves no time or place for these, and other, antiquated emotional distractions."

Fascinated, I read the whole little book quickly and then, realizing that my researching these ancient texts was not permitted, I became afraid that someone would catch me. I quickly buried the little book back in the box with the other books and clandestinely returned to my house and work. Unresolved fear and distress continued to overwhelm me, (which I hid very well from everyone,) as I worked at disciplining my mind to not think these thoughts anymore. Slowly over time, these questions, and this alienation, decreased and mostly went away. At some point I must have gone back to sleep and was no longer bothered by these existential questions. What a relief!

I never quite understood why I was born on Polonia and was quite relieved that, when I finally died and the doorway to the other side opened, I found Thomas standing there: my father and soul mate. What a joy it was being dead! I was so happy! We talked and talked, becoming absorbed in each other's spiritual force, waiting for our beloved Sandia to join us. I never quite figured out why or how we chose to incarnate on that ice world. Maybe we were born on Polonia so we could learn about our conflicted emotions by experiencing a life devoid of feeling. Maybe we were born there to take a small vacation from the unrelenting demand by Spirit for transformation. But it never really felt like a vacation. It was cold, and colder still was the closed heart. It was a world without love.

I think I learned that living in a world devoid of emotions, devoid of creative thinking, devoid of the kinds of traumatic hooks and conflicted knot of circumstances that plague most other worlds and most other lifetimes, that plague the story of the sentient experience, is not the path to transformation, is not an alternative to this messy human reality.

At least not for me.

Chapter 5 The Chariot

More than once I was born into the same peasant family living near the border with the Northwest Nation where there was a constant smuggling of rare and precious gems and metals through the forest from one country to another. I only knew about this because my mother's brother was somehow involved with the smuggling and there would be hushed conversations from time to time where these matters were obviously being discussed.

We lived near an old temple, buried deep in the forest, hidden from time and passerby. My mother was a religious person who made food offerings to the local religious community every day. The mendicants would come on their begging rounds each morning and she would have the most beautiful food prepared for them. I'm sure the word was out in that tribe of wanderers that my mother's house was a good place to go because each day a dozen or more robe-covered individuals would line up outside the side door of our house and be served their single meal of the day.

On festival days, the regular group of monks would be joined by dozens of temporary monks and nuns who would have taken the religious vows for three or seven days. The amount of food prepared and served during these festivals was huge. Not only did the resident and temporary monks and nuns eat, but afterwards the entire village ate as well. The food was always delicious and grand. There were more sweets and desserts on the end of the table than anyone, even the whole village, could eat but somehow it managed to be eaten. Some food was set aside for those monks and nuns who were too old or infirm to leave their rooms. But that was it.

For my mother, this was her entire life. Feeding the monks and taking care of the local temple was at once her work (she received some small donations) and a holy purpose- this path of service was a direct source of salvation for her. It always amazed me that these monks, who by religious practice ate only one meal a day, and basically performed few other worldly activities, had a whole community of people preoccupied with feeding them.

So, it came as no surprise to me, that, when I turned 12 years old, my mother brought me to the monastery and left me there. I should have known this would be my fate; I offered no resistance. I loved my mother very much and I didn't want to be away from her but, even so, I still had no idea how all-consuming my longing for her was to become over the years. I was never able to break this desire and attachment.

My father died suddenly in my twentieth year as a monk and I did not get the chance to share the last water with him. My sisters married and moved to other villages. Finally, my mother moved in with my elder brother and lived there comfortably with his family. I was only able see her on festival days. But I yearned to be in her presence every day, every day, and felt guilty and ashamed to be so attached after so many years practicing detachment. But this was what was true. For fifty years I hid this secret, and hid the guilt and shame that came with it.

One day in the middle of my 58th year as a monk (my 70th year) I received a message that my mother was near death and she requested my presence. I went immediately. When I walked into the room, she was lying in the bed, old and wrinkled. She said hello in a dry and weak voice; her breathing was irregular and difficult. I loved her so much then, in the human way, with human love, not just the detached universal love that I had spent a lifetime cultivating. I wanted to hold her, touch her one last time.

An incredible clarity shown through her eyes and the light emanating from her wrinkled face lit up the whole room. When I let my eyes go out of focus and examined the periphery of my sight, I saw many smaller lights darting from place to place around her body. When I let my ears go above and below the normal audible range I heard an ancient chant pulsating in the background. I became happy and deeply infused with love and had to breathe slowly and consciously to center my mind back in the present moment. But the chorus became louder, the smell of the lotus stronger, the darting light flashes brighter and more exhilarating.

I recited the Act of Truth, remembering threads of the multiple lives we had shared, the complex web of feeling and destiny that had infused our lives. I asked for forgiveness for any way I might ever have hurt her, might have hurt the person I loved most in the world. My mother looked at me and spoke softly in a dry and hoarse voice:

"Ro-ban, my sweet--," Ro-ban was her nickname for me. No one, including my mother, had addressed me that way since I had been ordained six decades ago. "Ro-ban, the gate has opened for me and my chariot is waiting. I must...go... now..." Her words were slow. Each word was a deep effort to utter. I could literally see her spirit body climbing into the chariot, strong and vital. She was sitting in the chariot now, looking at me with piercing eyes, making one last effort at speech.

"I will wait for you..... get ready..... so much to do..." she uttered finally.

My entire body was crying. Her chariot began to move, slowly at first, then faster. She glanced back one last time as her body became completely still, losing the remaining life force. I cried for a long time, not because I was sad. I was so happy. My entire experience became filled with happiness and light.

Something was different for me from then onward. My spiritual practice became very concentrated, my discipline very strong. I lived to a very old age, taught the sacred teachings to many people and when the dying time came, passed quickly with no suffering. In the last mind moments of consciousness, as my students gathered around the old and wrinkled body, a great light appeared in my mind. I recognized it immediately. It was my Saki's chariot. I leapt out of my robes and rushed to the empty seat beside her. We looked into each other's eyes, deeply, widely, happily.

Only a few seconds passed. Without speaking, we both knew what to do. In the next outbreath we jumped from the chariot, holding hands, our minds linked to the same point of light. Moments later we landed in the same womb, still holding hands, our eyes still locked on each other. Whether we were born holding hands, I do not actually remember. Probably not. Years later our mother said she knew the moment we had both come into her womb. She said she was six months pregnant and at home with our father watching a video. It was an old movie about the Olympics and the hero's struggle with faith and the victory of faith and love. The movie was called 'Chariots of Fire.' Somehow, this story always pleased us as children, and we made our mother tell it to us often.

Chapter 6. Xetex

Richard was parked outside the Xetex Instrument Company, waiting for Sarah to come out. He knew she worked late on Thursdays, having been told by her roommate that the best time to reach her was when she got off work on Thursday at 8:30 exactly. He was pacing back and forth near the curb, wanting her to see him immediately. Which she did. "Well Richard, what are ya doin' here?" Sarah asked surprised. "How'd ya know I'd be off work now.? What's goin' on? Are you stalking me?" she said playfully.

He didn't know where to begin. "Let's get some diiner, find a place where we can talk."

"Well I'm starved, Richard. Maybe we can get a bite to eat and you can tell me what's on your mind, whatever can be so important that you had to surprise me like this after work." She pointed to small Italian restaurant across the street from the Xetex Research Campus and they headed in that direction. It was a beautiful spring evening as they walked along the manicured paths, avoiding the sprinkler showers. Richard was silent as they walked. Sarah was apprehensive and walked quickly.

She thought to herself how much she liked him, but surprising her like this was a little strange, to say the least, and if this erratic behavior was typical she would have to say goodbye right away. She certainly didn't need another neurotic boyfriend.

They continued to walk in silence. Obviously something very serious was on Richard's mind, but it looked like he wanted to wait until they sat down at the restaurant before talking. Sarah tried some idle talk, just to break the ice, commenting on the beautiful spring weather.

"I love all these green lawns just after the rain," she said after a deep inhale. Just then a pair of sparrows came diving onto the lawn. They were dancing and flittering, hopping and chasing each other. Then they flew off. Richard and Sarah continued to walk along the manicured lawn paths, past the small high-tech buildings. The sun was very low in the sky and might have already set; Sarah couldn't tell. But the shadows were getting longer and very few people remained on the campus.

She thought of how she and Richard had met and gotten to know each other over the past several months. She had been working at Xetex for 5 years now, having graduated with combined degrees in biomedical and astromedical research. She had interned at Xetex in her senior year and merely continued in her job…except that now she was being paid for it. She thought it was important work: searching for biological indications in the terrestrial and extraterrestrial record. Finding life wherever it might be, whatever little corner or crevice of the natural world it might be hiding in. She was especially excited about the recently discovered habitats long buried under the polar icecaps on Earth. When the poles began melting, more and more land mass had been revealed below the ice. Frozen into the ground was an amazing biological record that included new DNA signatures not previously recorded. Some suggested there had been, at one time, a third DNA strand. Her work involved an equal amount of lab time, field work, computer modeling and team collaboration. Her coworkers were as committed as she was and the whole enterprise had this incredible expectancy. They all thought and believed that something very significant was going to come out of their work.

That was how she had met Richard: at a conference on Theoretical Bio-Physics in which Richard gave the opening Keynote. He was one of the new breed of scientists- not a specialist like she was- but a generalist in a world of micro specificity. While she had a lot more detailed information about exobiology, for example, Richard had a lot of interrelated information about multiple disciplines- from microbiology to quantum physics; from psychology to psychokinetics. His work involved synthesizing the manifold streams of data coming into the pool of common knowledge- from a cacophony of myriad, isolated. and specialized sources- and making some sense out of all that data. His science was not a science of specialty but a science of synthesis. It had been hundreds of years since any one person could know "everything there was to know," and while Richard certainly did not know "everything," his goal and objective was to bring the many fractured disciplines and mini-disciplines and mini-mini-disciplines and subsets of the micro disciplines into a form that could be made useful and understandable. He had written the bestseller, *A Simplified Theory of Everything*, and had been written up in the New York Times.

She had liked him immediately. He was fiercely intelligent but not arrogant. He was willing to listen, to change his ideas as new information came forward, but he was not ambivalent or unsure about those things that he knew. He knew what he knew. And he knew there was a great deal he didn't know. And he knew there was still a great deal that not anyone knew, that perhaps was not even knowable. She appreciated his humility while at the same time it impressed her that he could quote biblical passages as well as having memorized the entire database of the Genome Project. He knew the names and locations of hundreds of stars and galaxies. He knew the names and habitats of a broad spectrum of living creatures from South Pacific sea anemones to self-replicating bacteria living beneath what was left of the Arctic Ice Cap. Sometimes, she thought, all his knowledge must be a burden, at least it seemed like it should have been a burden, or, at least, would have been a burden for her if she were in his shoes, but he seemed not to be bothered by it. No, he seemed quite normal, actually, and quite adapted to his mission. So why was he suddenly acting so weird?

They arrived at the restaurant just then. The sun had set now, for sure. The clouds had turned from a red yellow to a blue gray. The sky beyond the clouds was still light: no stars were visible yet. A few cars travelled down the street; a few couples strolled past them as they made their way to the restaurant door. The outside tables were empty but it was a little too chilly to sit outside and they found their way to a table alongside the brick wall. The interior ambience was really quite pleasant; sawdust was liberally sprinkled on the floor and pictures of ancient Italian cities hung on the red brick walls.

These hanging pictures in themselves were amazing. They appeared to be high quality photographic images of ancient cities, cities long gone from the terrestrial historical record- Pompeii, Alexandria, Thebes, the Ziggurat of Ur and others. The photos looked like they were taken yesterday with high quality optics, and did not look like an artist's rendering. It really looked like someone had actually taken those pictures, as though someone had flown back in time with a new Nikon Digital and snapped the images of these lost cities. The tables themselves, on the other hand, were made of old barn wood planks, stained dark. The chairs were wrought iron and a little too uncomfortable. The lighting was fairly bright, as far as restaurants go- this was surely not a romantic getaway spot. It was where people hung out and drank beer after work. It was quiet, however, when they got there; the after work crowd was already gone. They were served immediately by the waitperson.

Sarah spoke first, as much to break the ice as to proceed with a normal conversation. She commented on the incredible photography on the walls. "It's always amazing to me how these photographs could possibly exist. I mean, they are so real, so tangible, so- so present. Looks like someone shot them just last week or last month. What do you think, Richard? How did they get such clear images of these no longer existing cities? How did they even know what they looked like in order to digitalize them so authentically to begin with?"

Richard thought for a moment. He knew the complex digital graphic technology that was involved. That was the easy part, known to many. He told her about the 'clairvoyants' who were able to travel in time and come back fully able to describe what they saw. "Incredible," was all she could say.

"There are so many incredible things, it just keeps blowing my mind, and that's after all my training in the grand themes of human knowledge," he said back to her. This was a familiar place and he could talk about these subjects for hours. But he had to bring the conversation back into focus, get to the matter at hand.

The food came just then. Bread with olive oil and some soup. Richard broke off a piece of bread, dipped it in the olive oil, ate it slowly and then began speaking.

"Sarah," he began, as present as he could be, but still very afraid, jittery with fear. "I have this overwhelming desire to be with you. Since we met, you have filled my thoughts with your shining face and your beautiful smile…"

"Richard, don't be weird…"

"I know this is rushed and, over time, maybe we could have gotten to know each other in a more normal way, but we don't have that much time, at least I don't. I have to be leaving in a few days and I don't know when I'll be back. I want you to know how much I love you, how much I've always loved you. I'm afraid I will lose contact with you and I won't have had the chance to tell you. I couldn't endure that again."

"Again?" Sarah interjected with a hesitant voice. "What do you mean--- again?"

"I feel like we're soulmates, coming together lifetime after lifetime… you must be able to feel it too?" he said with a pleading voice, half as a question, half as a fact.

Sarah was staring at him intently. He met her gaze and their eyes locked onto each other. And then, suddenly, in that moment, behind their eyes, their minds merged. Behind their minds, their souls embraced and suddenly, unexpectedly, there was a mutual instantaneous recognition of their connection and soul history. Their hearts opened fully and they smiled at each other.

The waiter came just then to take their order. The waiter, unaware of any of this, asked if they wanted to hear the dinner specials. That broke their concentration. Sarah looked down and away, almost embarrassed by the sudden intimacy. Richard looked up at the waiter.

"Two angel hair pasta with garlic sauce," Richard said coherently. "Is that o.k. with you, Sarah?"

"Yes, please." she answered, pretending coherence. The waiter took the menus and left quickly. Richard took another piece of bread. Sarah spoke first.

"That was amazing… did you see what I saw? Did you feel that?" It was like asking someone in the same room after a 6.5 earthquake whether they felt any shaking.

"I've been feeling this way ever since we met." Richard replied quickly. "Sarah, I feel so connected… when our eyes met, something happened. I felt like our souls merged…"

"It was amazing!"

"That's what I'm trying to say, I've been feeling this way since we first met. And now you say you feel it too. Then I must not be crazy after all," he said, almost triumphantly, but with a sense of relief also.

Sarah looked pensive, staring into the distance at the holographic art on the walls, just beyond Richard's head. She realized that Richard was not the stranger she had thought he was. Her fear and apprehensiveness were suddenly gone and she saw that she trusted him, something that was hard for her to do.

"This sure was a surprise. I thought we were going to have dinner and you were going to tell me some dark secret, but here we are, revealed to each other as long time lovers, best friends and soul mates. Wow!" joyfully exclaimed Sarah.

"So what was it you were going to tell me, actually? What was so important that you had to have this clandestine dinner with me after working late today?" Sarah asked playfully. Richard, also playfully, replied, "Just to tell you that I really, really, love you."

Chapter 7 Chariot2

My sister and I grew up in an affluent community in a big city. My father worked for a multinational and would often be gone for weeks and even months at a time. He was working on a large construction project in Irodios, somewhere in the desert of the Middle North, having been hired by the king of that country to create a new inland sea, complete with waves and tides and beachfront.

My father had helped design powerful 3rd generation solar devices that harnessed the desert sun and could generate enough energy to condense the loose hydrogen in the atmosphere. This super-saturated hydrogen was used as the power source to make normal drinking and irrigation water and now, with the recently developed boson generator, an inland sea. As a child I only knew that my father was involved in terraforming the Northern desert, making a sea where only sand dunes had existed. Mostly, I knew that he was gone a lot, but we had reconciled ourselves to him being gone because he was doing something so important.

Once a week, on the telescreen in the library room, we would visit with our father. Precisely at 8:00 on Friday, we would sit around the room and wait for the geo-satellite connection to synch up with the holographic projector. Then my sister, my mother, and I would sit around and have a conversation with him, as though he were right there with us. We showed him the various school projects we had done; he would show us panoramic video of the desert that was slowly being lasered and transformed into an inland sea. From time to time, we would have other family and other visitors attend our weekly get together.

My twin sister and I grew up very proud of our father, but missing him terribly. Our mother, Maryanne, did everything for us. She seemed so strong, so sufficient and capable. Now, as an old man retrieving this memory from the akashic record, I find it remarkable how well she actually did, given the competing demand on her love life by who was then my father's best friend, Nicolas. Nicolas seemed like a great friend for my mother, helping her out, driving us kids here and there. We were never surprised to see him in the house; in fact, we liked having Nicolas around. Over the years while our father worked on Irodios- say from when we were 6 until about 15- Nicolas was very present in the household. Curiously, and I never really noticed this at the time, he somehow always seemed to be gone on those Friday nights when we would sit around with our father on the wide holographic screen.

Of course, by the time my sister and I were of age to understand these things, after she and I had moved to the Far Continent to continue our schooling, my mother married Nicolas. Our father, who by this time had long completed the "Irodios Desert Reclamation" project, was very distraught over this and spent the rest of his life living as a recluse in the Irodios mountain range known as Rock Water. I think he never forgave our mother or Nicolas and, as far as I can tell, the three of them began a roll through time working that out. How many lifetimes, how many births and deaths, I don't know. From my own experience, these kinds of things take a long time. For me it has taken ten thousand years.

It's a funny thing, but even through the great changes in technology, the great achievements in human history, the great evolution of the sentient biogram, the human condition and human nature remain the same. On all the various planes and planets where we reside and collect experience, whether in the cave or on a spaceship, the core foundation of human experience doesn't really change. We love, we want to be loved; we desire, we possess, we lose our way, we find our way.

One wonders why, why do we go through this roller coaster ride, this sentient experience? Why do we go through the pain, the suffering, again and again? Why get on the ride at all; why not stay in the backfield, on the sidelines, in the subtle planes of existence where this craziness appears more like an aberration then a cosmic necessity? This is a tough question.

The answer is: Here we are, right now, breathing, thinking, feeling consciousness. Consciousness with Form. Consciousness with Will. The Universe- biologic nature, galactic nature, even the dark matter wormholes- everything that happens, everything that exists- is an incredibly efficient machine that automatically creates form from our thoughts to the degree that our thoughts are infused with feelings and intention. Individually as well as collectively, nothing is wasted, nothing is extra: there are no ruffles on the pillow case. Our life, our suffering, our happiness, our redemption, our enlightenment must be necessary for the process of creation to proceed. We are a piece of the grander puzzle; we are, and our experience is, necessary for the universe to happen.

Sara and I spent the next 130 solar years living an ordinary life. We were both married, had children, struggled with our feelings, with the affairs of daily living. Although our ten thousand years of sentience may have helped us sort through the complicated quagmire of day to day existence, we were still subject to its laws- conflict, decay, and change, as well of course as love and friendship and truth and beauty. About 10 years after our mother died, we both became involved with a small school that trained individuals in the healing arts. Notwithstanding the great advances in medical and psychotherapeutic technology, there was, and always will be, at these sentient planes of existence, a need for healing and transformation.

I died first. There were no fancy chariots this time, no disciples to grieve, no unfinished business in some old monk's account book. Sara came pretty soon after. Tendo was already there. We embraced each other, merged our soul bodies into the one spirit, showering in the rays of the central sun and healing the core thread. We talked for a bit about our experiences in physical form, about the feelings and sensations that over-whelmed our senses. We laughed about some of the silly karmic subrou-tines we kept running. And we cried and held each other, remembering the complex quagmires of loyalty and devotion, of love and betrayal that we continuously created. We reminisced about all the good times, tried to forget all the bad times. But still, even having gone through the fire again and again, having tasted the bitterness inherent in the very fabric, at the center of being alive, there was still something so utterly compelling about physical experience, something utterly and indescribably delicious about sentient life, that even after having collected every type of experience ten times over, we still, in the end, wanted more. We wanted to be alive! It was amazing!

We thought about going back, even starting in the caves again and going through the entire journey, and who knows, maybe we might still. But there was a long line waiting to get on the roller coaster and, hey, it was someone else's turn.

Epilogue

At first Ladro thought it was a machine glitch. He would be the first to admit that he had become complacent over the last few hundred thousand years. Standing inside the Generator Building, at the center of the massive array of vibrating neo-hyper metal and plastic conduits, Ladro is staring intensely at his calculator. Something is wrong. He shakes it, turns the power button off and then back on, shakes it again. He moves over to his central terminal display, hits some buttons and hastily enters a detailed algorhythm. The neon tubes pulsate brightly for a few moments but soon resume their original depleted color and intensity. He makes additional entries into his terminal, moving his hands wildly in front of the holographic display. Neuro-ganglia begin to extend out from the core processor disappearing into the extensive virtual hologram miniaturized on the wall monitor array for everyone to see. A crowd of neo-techs stand in awe watching the master manipulate the Cosmic Engine.

"Shit," he yells out in frustration. "Could someone check the fucking batteries?" as dozens of acolytes race around in disarray. Nothing seems to work. The neon tubes continue to dim.

Aung walks into the main control room just as Ladro has thrown his coffee cup at the terminal display. Broken ceramic glass and coffee grinds are splattered everywhere. Ladro is standing in front of the nucleonic sub-quark transponder muttering obscene words in hundreds of languages at once. It is a cacophony of adolescent slang mixed with sarcastic epithets and undigested spittle. Ladro is beside himself.

He sees Aung and angrily points to the holographic quark-sized protonic conductors a few feet to the left. He mumbles additional epithets while continuing to point a finger at Aung.

"It's all your fault, you and your stupid sentients, the stupid creatures who you cared so much about, whose suffering bothered you so much that you had to change the whole goddamn fucking fabric of existence to allow them to…what?…not suffer?…" he said with disdain, uttering the next words with a huge contempt and exaggerated flamboyance, "…to get liberated, la di da, to get enlightened? So as not to suffer, la di da, just so you didn't have to feel so bad or work so hard. You self-righteous narcissist. You only cared about how bad you felt, how hard it was for you. You didn't care about my job, what I had to do, what the Creator told me was important. No, you didn't care about the big picture, about the continuity of existence. No, you had to do it your way. I knew I should never have listened."

Ladro went back to his Level Nine switches, turning this and re-arranging that but the neon tubes continued to decrease in size. Aung, obviously distressed at seeing his old friend flip out, was nonetheless quite happy. What it meant was that the process of Awakening, of Creation Knowing Itself, had taken root in the fabric of sentient existence and could no longer be dislodged. It had become embedded inside the sub nuclear matrix and had transformed the nature of existence itself. He had achieved the Creator's hidden goal of eliminating sentient suffering.

Actually, Aung really was quite proud of himself and, though Ladro's angst and anger were a painful and distressing side product, he was quite happy underneath the feigned concern he pretended to Ladro. Of course, Ladro knew immediately that Aung was patronizing him.

"You're despicable Aung! You pretend to be such a good boy, but because of your 'good' work, everything that makes you so proud and arrogant, the entire Creation will come to a halt. Don't you see that, you moron, you self-centered hypocrite? Instead of helping the Creator, now you have thwarted the Creator's will." Ladro would have gone on, but Aung turned away.

He looked around. Where was the Creator now that he had accomplished the task He had set for him. Why doesn't He tell Ladro to back off, make Ladro quiet down, see the beauty in a self-aware universe: a holy place where peace and joy and not greed and hatred are the basis of experience, a place where the sentients have become liberated from the condition of universal discontent that was the automatic consequence of an object and desire-centered world. He glanced over at the fuming Ladro. "Don't worry, little brother, the Creation is not going to die out for a long time. You still have the energy of recycled death to power up your machine. Everything still dies and that energy is more than enough to keep it going for a very long time and…"

"Don't little brother me, you stupid idiot. As the Universe has expanded so much since the beginning of Creation, the whole thing is so much larger now, occupying so many more nanogigs of space, that the amount of energy released at death is, at this point, totally insufficient. We have become dependent on that specific energy stream, generated from the sentient layer of the fabric, to sustain the whole thing. Where have you been? We've studied these equations down to the smallest quark micron; whole cosmic think tanks have been set up to optimize these energy conduits. Didn't you read the fuckin' memos? Nobody has a solution, nobody- so don't you come in here and give me your optimistic little brother bullshit!!!." screamed Ladro in front of the assembled acolytes.

Slowly, and more slowly, the engine continues to slow down. Agonizingly, Ladro tries some last minute tactics. He initiates terrible wars on multiple worlds, hoping that that might distract the sentients from their obsession with ascension and transformation. On many worlds he convinces the younger souls that their personal worth, and their source of happiness and purpose in life, was measured in the accumulation of shiny metal objects which Ladro hoped would make them abandon their inspiration for awakening and knowing.

On other worlds he caused huge destruction of habitat, created planet-wide famines and disturbed natural cycles. Centuries of intergalactic wars killed billions of sentient, resulting in a huge uptick of death and suffering energy.

But, alas, it was not enough. A small spike showed up in the master ion matrix, some additional photonic fibers rose out of the central Generator, but it was not enough. Ladro knew it wouldn't be. The wave of liberated energy was a huge tsunami, unstoppable in the cosmic mindfield.

Ladro is now sitting near the main entrance to the Generator. His calculator is in his hand but there are no lights flashing. He appears dejected and depressed. "All is lost now. I've failed in my task- there's no hope now...," he moans, in between sobs. "I've let the Creator down. He told me to sustain Creation at all costs, and now, look at this, Creation is nearing its end. I have failed. This is horrible."

Aung tried to focus on his desperate friend. "The Creator must have designed it this way- it can't have been left up to you- or me. I mean, He is the Creator and this is His Creation. He must have meant for this to happen. It has to have been built into it..." replied Aung, distressed at seeing the once mighty and proud Ladro reduced to a whimper and cry. "It isn't your fault. Didn't you say, when the Creator brought in the sentient formula, that He had gone off to...somewhere.? Where did he go? You said he came back sad and unhappy." Aung thought that maybe

Ladro would see that the Creator had always had this intent, to wind it down, to get to the end point so He could see Her.

Ladro, broken now, was about to say something back to Aung when suddenly the space between the molecules shuddered and there, standing next to Ladro and Aung was the Creator, resplendent and all powerful, crystallized into a magnificent human-like form. Ladro and Aung became transfixed, bowing gracefully and with deep feeling.

"It's slowing down and will soon stop. The sustaining of this Creation has ceased," he said out loud to Ladro and Aung and, presumably, all orders of celestial beings. "We're almost there now, only a few seconds…" He continued. Of course, a few seconds was also a very long time on the various planets and planetoids spread across cosmic space. But nonetheless, those few seconds passed in transcendent and profound silence and suddenly, suddenly it stopped: just like that. Everything just stopped. Creation came to a halt. The moons and stars and planets, everything from the tiniest sub-nuclear quark to the largest spiral mega-galaxy, all stopped moving, devibrating themselves out of existence.

Ladro was beside himself. All these aeons of work, all the multi-millennia of trans galactic time, all the ponderous and traumatizing moments negotiating the errorless functioning of the Cosmic Generator- all this for naught! It was over!!! That all there was to it, it was just over ?!!!

Aung, on the other hand, stood there fixated, his attention on the small wave-like distortion in the field above and behind the Creator's head. Ladro was ranting and raving, screaming at the celestial beings who, like Aung, were watching the space around the Creator's head, mesmerized.

As the Creator completed the final push of His out-breath, then, in that singular empty moment, where Creation and all of existence is poised to return upon itself in the immanent and inevitable in-breath, but just before He actually made the first flicker of a movement, in the timelessness between the breaths, in the singular instant where time stops and before it begins flowing in a different direction, there appeared standing next to the Creator the most wondrous Divine Being that could be imagined. Not just another Celestial Deity, another Angel or Divine Goddess, it was… the same as the Creator, except more wonderful, more beautiful, more utterly and totally Divine. The Creatrix. She stood in front of the celestial choir, resplendent, glorious and happy.

The Creator spoke first. "You didn't have to come here. I asked you not to …" He said to Her, softly, tears running down His face.

"I had to be with you, here where time stands still." She said back to Him, also softly, with tears running down Her face. "I have waited this whole eternity to be near you, look into your eyes again, touch your hand…,"

They embraced and in their embracing a light emanated from their joined hearts, exploding outward, flooding all the channels and conduits of the Cosmic Mind. Light filled up all Space with Deep Love and every being that had ever existed was instantly freed from darkness and all the realms of existence were liberated and set free.

After what seemed like a very long time, They relaxed from Their embrace. Where a moment ago the profound immanence of Love and Transcendent Joy was so thick that it transformed the entire Cosmos, now a sadness began to overwhelm all those that watched. Transparent to everyone, in front of the celestial choir, He grasped at Her, tried to pull Her closer, unwilling to let go of the embrace.

Her expression turned from Love and Joy to sadness as well. "I must be going now," She sobbed.

"No, don't go. Stay with me…don't go…" the Creator pleaded quietly.

"You know I have to go. I'm not finished dancing. You know I have to go… Maybe I should not have come here now. I didn't want to hurt you, but…but I couldn't wait- I just couldn't wait to be near you again, if even just for a moment. I'm so happy," She said, crying profusely.

They both stood there embracing, next to Ladro's broken Generator, the prime Singularity in the middle of Emptiness. "We are never apart," She whispered.

"I Am Thee," He whispered back.

"Wait for me" She cried as Her voice began to trail off. "Sustain me, protect me, hold my world, watch over my children…"

Suddenly, the entire cosmos shuddered. And She was gone. The Creator stood there looking off into the distance. Very sad. His mouth looked like He was talking but no words came out. He became sadder and sadder.

Finally, after a very, very long moment, He began a long deep inhale… …and disappeared.

Finale

He said "And so it's done now, this world has come and gone."
She said "O Lord, what joy it was, to bring Thee into form."
He said "So beautiful, the moons and stars, that filled the stellar night."
She said "And because I love this world, You filled it with your Light."

He said to Her "But your children, their life and death, is born of our desire-
our love, our lust, our longing, is the fuel of that mortal fire."
She said to Him "That pain and woe, so deep and cruel, too much for me to bear,"
She cried aloud "Too many lives, and too much time, lost in suffering and despair."

He said to Her "O sweet Divine, let's dance a different Dance."
She said to Him "A sweeter dream, more love and hope- maybe there's a chance-
We can make a world that has no Death, a world that has no Night."
He said to Her "I'll dream a world where you can Dance, a Dance of pure white Light."

Then He said "Let me hold you now, make love to you all day."
She said "And you are mine to hold, to dream with while we play"
And now He held Her tight and firm
In the matrix of His mind.
And She held Him softly inside Her heart
beyond the edge of time.

The End